IT'S A
Vampire
CHRISTMAS

VAMPIRE LORDS
BOOK ONE

LIA DAVIS

It's A Vampire Christmas
Vampire Lords, book 1
By: Lia Davis

Published by After Glows
© 2015 Lia Davis

ISBN: 978-0-9908867-1-6

Cover Art by Charity Hendry
Formatting by Inkstain Interior Book Designing

The hunt for the past will set their future...
Alasdair Morgan, vampire lord of the south Atlantic region of
the United States, and his mate, Gideon, are on the search for
an ancient journal. The secrets the book holds within its leather
binding can be used to destroy their race's queen, Lilith. When
they finally find the journal, they discover it has been sold to an
antique store. However, a female with her own agenda has her
sights set on possessing the book.

Some gifts come in twos...
Being a half-breed living among humans, Rhianna Howell
knows the importance of secrecy all too well. When she
discovers one of the lost vampire artifacts, she doesn't waste
time in collecting it before it falls into the wrong hands. But
keeping the journal safe from evil will put her in the seductive
path of two vampires who claim to be her mates.
The days and nights heat up this Christmas as she discovers a
fiery passion she can't deny or run from.

OTHER BOOKS BY LIA DAVIS:

For the inner vamp in us all…

Chapter 1

"I FOUND IT."

Alasdair glanced up from his computer as Gideon, his best friend and lover, burst through the mahogany double doors of the study, tablet in hand and a brilliant smile on his handsome face. The bright gleam of excitement in the other vampire's gaze sparked Alasdair's own. Could it be? After two centuries of searching, had the journal been found?

Gideon's light brown hair hung in his eyes as he crossed the white tile floor. He stopped in front of the desk. When their gazes locked, Alasdair knew the male had indeed found the book. Alasdair held his hand out and the other male handed over the tablet. The image on the screen, though fuzzy, was identical to the leather-bound journal he'd been searching for. He was sure of it. He'd spent many nights of his youth reading the stories his grandmother wrote of her life. The Morgan family crest—a crouching gargoyle with the letter M in an elegant calligraphy overlaid him like a brand—on the cover appeared to be correct, but it was hard to tell due to the poor quality of the photo.

There was no doubt in Alasdair's heart that the book in the picture was his great grandmother's diary. "You did it." He met Gideon's stare, a hint of sadness clouding the blue depths. "What?"

Gideon dropped into the chair across from the desk. The morning light filtering in through the large window behind Alasdair caught the natural blond highlights in Gideon's hair beautifully. Alasdair's hands itched to comb through the silken strands, and reward his lover for finding the journal.

"Where is it?"

"I traced it to an antique shop In New York."

Fuck. "I'll call Julian and get clearance for you to fly right away."

"Wouldn't that take too long? Couldn't you have Julian run down to get it?"

"Julian doesn't run to get anything. He may be like a brother to me, but he doesn't do anything himself. I don't trust anyone but you to collect the journal." Alasdair picked up his phone and pressed the New York vampire lord's number.

Julian picked up on the second ring. "To want do I owe this wonderful surprise, Al?"

Gritting his teeth, Alasdair let the taunt go. He didn't have time to play games with Julian. "I need to fly my consort to your territory tonight."

A bitter, humorless laugh filtered through the phone. "It's a little late notice. What business do you have here?"

One. Two... "There's an artifact he needs to collect for me."

"It can't wait?"

"No."

Silence fell over the line for several long moments. "What type of artifact?"

"A family heirloom."

"Ah, I see. Are you certain?" Julian was one of the few who knew about the journal and its significance to the history of their race. It was only one of several artifacts that had been hidden from Lilith's sister, Violet, about eight hundred years ago.

"Yes. Gideon found it online just a few moments ago." Alasdair met Gideon's gaze. His lover's fangs peaked from beneath his upper lip and his hands fisted over the arms of his chair. A low growl rumbled from him. Gideon was annoyed with the vampire lord. Alasdair also grew impatient. If it wasn't so critical to retrieve the journal, he'd tease his old friend about his superior attitude. With a shake of the head, Alasdair held up a finger in warning.

"It's Grandmother's," he said, allowing irritation to leak out in his tone. Alasdair let his head fall back against the headrest of his chair. Julian, along with every vampire lord, knew his great grandmother Annamarie was one of the first vampires created by Lilith over five thousand years ago. The other lord also understood that any artifact belonging to Annamarie was very important.

After a long pause, Julian sighed. "Gideon is the only one allowed to come. He's to gather this artifact and leave within three days." A click sounded over the line, indicating the conversation was over.

Alasdair placed the phone on the desk, and met Gideon's stare. "Watch your back. Bless will be watching you and I don't have to tell you what a bitch she is."

Bless was Julian's right hand and one of his best sentries. She loved to play on others' fears. Especially Gideon's since it was a female gargoyle that had ended his human life.

A wicked smile formed on the Gideon's lips. "I know how to deal with Bless. Besides she will be in stone while I retrieve the journal."

Gideon had an easygoing charm about him, one of the many traits Alasdair loved about the male. "Please be sure to hurry. We can't afford for the journal to fall into Violet's hands." *Besides, I will miss you.* Alasdair pushed away the insecurity and cursed himself for the weakness.

As if sensing his train of thought, Gideon rose from his chair, paced to Alasdair's side, and sat on the desk in front of him. He lowered his head and cupped Alasdair's chin, tilting his head up to claim his lips. Alasdair groaned and thrust his tongue inside his mate's mouth, savoring every brush of his tongue. Gideon tasted of scotch and a hint of blood.

Breaking the kiss, he fisted a hand in Gideon's brown hair. Alasdair gently tugged his head to the side then pressed his lips to the base of the male's throat. His lover's groan made Alasdair's dick jerk to attention. "Do hurry back. Our bed will be cold without you in it."

"Yes," Gideon breathed.

"Go gather your things and I'll alert the pilot." Alasdair reluctantly released the other male and watched him exit the study, wishing he could go. He couldn't leave Destin. Not with a pending war between vampires and earth bound demons stirring. Lilith had grounded all lords to their territories.

After hanging up with the pilot, his phone chimed to indicate a text message. He glanced at it and smiled. It was Rayne, Lilith's only daughter.

I would like to request permission to discuss the treaty.

In recent weeks, Lilith had sent her natural born children out to petition the lords to pledge their alliance to her. Violet, the queen's sister had started rallying groups of demons around the US as if preparing for an attack. Alasdair was sure the demon queen was doing just that. The sisters hated each other, and Violet would do anything to destroy the peaceful life Lilith and the other lords worked hard to build.

The lords had always been free to rule their territories independent from Lilith. But after signing the treaty, all laws and punishments would go through Lilith. No more independent territories. The terms were non-negotiable, and if a lord failed to comply, he or she would be deemed a rogue and put down.

Some thought it was harsh, but Alasdair, along with Julian and a few others, agreed it was time to strengthen their defenses and band together. The queen would have full access to their territories and sentries. *Something that should had happened a long fucking time ago.*

He texted back. *Of course princess, I look forward to the meeting.*

Likewise. Rayne returned.

He laughed, imagining her eye roll with the text message. She hated being referred to as *princess*. All the lords knew it, but they loved irritating her. Mostly because they watched her grow up and considered her as a sister.

Closing the messaging app, he rose and left his study to see Gideon off. Memories of the day he found his consort entered his mind as he padded through the foyer to the great room. The white tile floor, tan leather couch, and matching chairs were in complete contrast to the dark alley where he'd first found Gideon. The male had been human then, and dying. Something about him pulled at Alasdair's heart and soul. At the time he didn't know what it was, but when he approached his queen about the male, she'd explained it was a mating urge and that his soul had called out to the human.

After she had confirmed the male was of the right bloodline, she granted permission to have Gideon changed. Alasdair's chest tightened at the memories. Gideon was his first turn, his lover, and best friend. The thought of him being so far away increased Alasdair's anxiety, but at the same time excitement swirled at the knowledge of holding grandma's journal.

He crossed the room and met Edmond, one of the *echo* demons and the only one who lived in the main house. Alasdair kept his coven fairly small. There was the mansion and four smaller cottages—two on either side of the house—where a few of the vampires he turned and a family of echoes lived.

The echo had Gideon's duffle bag over one shoulder as he waited. Alasdair gave him a short nod and said, "Good afternoon, Edmond."

Nodding, Edmond offered a wide smile. "Hello, my lord. Gideon is leaving us for a while?" The demon's brows bunched as he studied his folded hands in front of him.

Alasdair patted him on the shoulder. "Just for a few days. But you know what I need you to do for me?"

Edmond glanced up, eyes bright with purpose. "What do you wish of me?"

Demon lords of hell had created *Echoes* for the sole purpose of serving. A few escaped into the human realm over the past several millennia. Lilith took them under her protection and many *echoes* served the vampire lords today. Edmond had served Alasdair's grandmother, Annamarie, and had remained loyal to the Morgan family ever since.

"Could you find out where Marie disappears to every couple of weeks?"

Edmond's gaze grew round and his hands started to shake. "Marie, sire?"

"Yes. If you know something you should tell me."

Nodding vigorously, he spoke in rush. "She sneaks off to see a male."

Alasdair blinked, a mixture of surprise and concern swirled in his mind. He fisted his hands at his side and suppressed the urge to growl at the *echo*. "What type of male? Do you know him?"

"I...no, sire. I don't know him. He's a vampire. From what I saw of him, he appears to be around Gideon's age." Edmond shifted from foot to foot, clearly sensing Alasdair's irritation.

Gideon approached from the stairs, and Alasdair breathed deeply as his lover's scent flowed around him. Meeting Gideon's serious gaze, Alasdair relax a little.

"What is it?" Gideon asked as he stopped next to him.

"Marie has been sneaking off to meet a vampire not from my coven."

Gideon shook his head. "She's young, Alas."

"That doesn't excuse her from not telling me. She has to understand that if he hurts her in anyway, I will kill him." Alasdair took a deep breath. Marie was his newest vampire, but she was smart and well aware of the rules. "She should know better than to sneak around."

He'd have to deal with Marie later. At the moment he had to send his love off to New York to collect Annamarie's journal before it fell into the wrong hands.

Gideon closed the small gap between them, and cupped Alasdair's cheek. "Always the protector. You'd make a wonderful father."

"Gideon—"

The other male pressed his lips to Alasdair, cutting off the words he'd spoken many times before. No matter how long they had searched, the perfect female to complete them wasn't out there. Alasdair had given up finding a third, a female who could share her life with them, love them, and bear their children.

When Gideon broke the kiss, he whispered. "She's out there. I feel it. Please be patient a little longer."

Closing his eyes, Alasdair nodded. He'd give Gideon anything. Hell, Alasdair was just as desperate to find a female to complete the union. Most matings developed a strong, unbreakable bond. However, the strings linking he and Gideon's seemed faint, almost transparent, like the Fates had something else in store for them.

"I'm not giving up, my love. But I am growing weary of searching."

"We'll find her," he said again before drawing him into a tight embrace. "I'll return as soon as I can. It's too damned cold in New York right now for me."

Laughing, Alasdair let go of his lover to take his duffle bag, and led the way to the waiting car. "Call me as soon as you land."

With a nod, Gideon climbed in and shut the door.

As Alasdair watched his partner leave, an icy sensation shivered up his spine. A vision he hadn't had in decades entered his mind. A beautiful woman with chestnut brown hair cascading over her shoulders stood in the middle of a room dressed in a long, white gown, her belly swollen with child.

His chest tightened and he shook off the vision. There had been a time when hope was strong in his heart. He and Gideon had used his gift of visions, deciphering them for clues to find her. But Alasdair was tired of the dead ends and the disappointments. The visions were no more than dreams. A false sense of their happily ever after.

Turning on his heels, he stormed into the house and toward his study. He would no longer search for an illusion of what the future may hold. No more wasting time and energy chasing a ghost.

Chapter 2

RHIANNA ENTERED THE small antique store and shivered. Damn, it was cold. The sun's only job this time of year was to provide light. It surely didn't warm things up. The icy wind cut through her knee-length wool coat as she made the three-block walk from her New York apartment building. With Christmas being three days away, the dry streets were littered with last minute shoppers, rushing from store to store and fighting over sales. Normally, she'd keep her ass at home and stay there until after New Year's, but she couldn't resist searching through the shop's latest treasures.

The antique store was bigger than it appeared. Year of buying and collecting old things made the owners expand to the second floor. What used to be an old studio apartment, now held furniture and other household trinkets. They even had appliances dating as far back as the early eighteen hundreds. The ground floor was where the less valuable, but still pretty cool items from the nineteen hundreds were displayed.

She passed an old fifties model jukebox on her way to the counter. She made a mental note to check it out next time, when she wasn't on her own little treasure hunt.

When she spoke to the owner a few days ago, he'd said they were going to an estate sale and would be bidding on some very old books and jewelry. Her interest had spiked at the news and she was eager to see what they brought back. So here she was, risking being trampled by holiday shoppers and freezing to death along the way.

And why? The spark of hope she had finally found her grandfather's talisman—a powerful one-of-a-kind amulet—was too great for her to ignore.

"Excuse me."

"Huh? Oh, sorry." Lost in thought, she didn't realize she was standing in the doorway like an idiot. "I'm Rhianna. I spoke with the owner the other day about a new shipment that was coming in today."

The girl smiled. "Yes, Mark said you'd be coming in and not to put anything out until you got here." She hopped off her stool. "Follow me, please."

Rhianna followed her behind a curtain. Her heartbeat increased the closer she got to the three large boxes in front of her. A slight tingle of magic drifted from the middle one. *It's got to be the amulet.*

The bell on the front door dinged and the girl motioned to the boxes. "Go ahead and have a look. I'll be right back."

Rhianna nodded but didn't remove her gaze from the box. Once the clerk left, Rhianna stepped forward and peered inside and frowned. The container was full of books. *Well, Damn.* Yet, the magic she'd felt when first entering the back room was stronger. With a quick glance over her shoulder to make sure the girl had left, she turned back to the box. Holding her hand over it, she whispered, "Come to me."

The books shook within the container. A leather bound volume levitated up to her hand. She grabbed it and walked to a metal folding chair and sat. After closer inspection she discovered it wasn't just any book, but an old hand written journal. By the yellowed, fragile parchment pages and the thinned, worn leather binding, she guessed it dated back to the early 16th century.

The cover had some kind of crest on the front, but it was too worn to clearly make out. She carefully opened the cover and gasped. On the first page, in faded handwriting, was a name she recognized from her father's history lessons.

Annamarie Morgan—one of the first vampires created by Lilith over five thousand years ago.

Holy, shit. She gently closed the book and darted out of the storeroom. "Miss? How much for this book?"

The girl faced her, glanced at the book, and shrugged. "Not sure. Mark will be here in about an hour."

No time. "I just realized I'm late for an appointment. I'll give you fifty dollars for it. If Mark wants more for it, just tell him to call me."

The clerk's eye widened. "That's a lot for an old book, but sure. I guess."

If only the girl knew how priceless the journal was. She paid the clerk and rushed down the sidewalk to her penthouse.

When she reached her building, she groaned at the sight of her father stepping out of his limo. You'd think a vampire would be a little less flashy. Not Julian Delacroix.

Put on your happy face, Rhi.

Smiling, she greeted the vampire who raised her. "What a wonderful surprise?"

He kissed her cheek and offered his arm to her. "Someone is much too happy to see me."

"I'm always happy to see you." She looped her arm in his.

Once in the elevator, Julian turned to her. "Did you find it?"

She sagged against the wall. "No. I'll keep looking though. It has to show up somewhere."

He gave a short nod as the door *swished* open. Rhianna stepped out into the large private foyer and unlocked her door. The heels of her boots clicked against the tile floor as she led her father into the apartment. "Would you like anything to drink?"

"Glass of wine, please." He removed his coat and hung it on the coatrack. "I don't understand why you don't have an *echo* here to help you?"

Pulling two stem-less wine glasses out of the cabinet, she rolled her eyes. "I don't need help. Besides your *echoes* don't like me."

"They like you. Your magic just intimidates them."

She grabbed a bottle of red wine from the rack and rounded the corner to the living room. Her father stood in front of the wall of glass overlooking the city. "You have the most beautiful view."

"You're not moving in," she teased.

He turned and smiled wide at her. Then held out his arms. She walked into them and allowed him to hug her close. "I've missed you."

"I've been home for four years."

"Yes, but you were involved." He tone held a hint of anger, though it wasn't directed toward her, and a hint of sadness.

Lifting on her toes, she kissed his cheek and moved out of his embrace. "I'm not discussing Charles. Every time I do, I want to kill something."

"Yes, I understand the feeling." He laughed as he followed her to the sofa then took the bottle from her.

She sat and watched him as he poured the wine, and handed her a glass. Taking a sip, she sank into the soft leather with a sigh. She didn't work and didn't need to thanks to the trust fund Julian set up for her when she was an infant. So she spent her days researching and tracking Violet's activities. "I found something this morning."

His gaze snapped up to hers and one brow lifted. "What?"

"Violet has moved south to Alabama, close to the gulf."

"Are you certain?" He tapped the side of his glass with his ring.

"Yes. I had Bless verify it. I'm surprised she hasn't already mentioned it."

"She might not think it's a big concern."

Rhianna let out a low growl. "Would the vampire lord in that region know?"

Nodding, he sipped his wine before replying. "I'll let him know. Speaking of Alasdair, his mate will be in town for a few days. I thought you should know in case you notice an out of town vampire wandering around."

"Wandering around?" She frowned, her thoughts returning to the journal. "He doesn't have business with you?"

One broad shoulder rose in a lazy shrug before he replied. "He's looking for an old book. Some kind of family heirloom. I've known Gideon since his turn. He's harmless... mostly."

She let out a breathy laugh at her father's attempt of a joke while hiding the spike in her pulse. "Thanks for letting me know."

She forced herself to remain calm and not give away the slow panic building inside her. The vampire was there to get the journal. And he'd hunt it down. *Damn.*

Chapter 3

A **CHIME SOUNDED** as Gideon entered the antique store, and drew his leather coat tighter around him. *Freakin' New York and their cold ass winters.* He strode to the counter where a young girl was handing change to a customer. Waiting until she was done and the man left the store, Gideon offered her a smile.

"I was hoping you could help me." He pulled out his phone and brought up the screen shot of the journal and faced it to her. "I was told your store bought this book from an estate sale recently."

She studied the photo for a moment. "Yes, we had a book that looked like that one."

His stomach soared. "You had?"

Her head bobbed up and down. "Just sold it."

Fuck. "Oh. That's unfortunate."

Glancing up, she met his stare and he took the opportunity to enter her most recent thoughts, a talent vampires developed over time. The slightly rounded face of a brunette with large brown eyes came into sight —

Rhianna Howell. The name was a whisper of a thought as if the store clerk knew the woman.

Withdrawing from the girls' thoughts, Gideon smiled, allowing it to reach his eyes. "Thank you for your help."

He left the store before the clerk had a chance to reply, and dialed Alasdair's number as he made his way through the sea of shoppers. Gideon didn't give the other vampire time to greet him. "Someone bought the book before I got here."

"Fuck."

"My thought exactly. However, I do have a name and plan to hunt her down."

Alasdair growled. "Hurry. If that book falls into Violet's hands—"

"It won't. I'll get the journal if I have to seduce the female into giving it to me." Gideon hoped he could just use a little vampire charm and steal the book, then leave town before she knew what happened.

There was a long pause before Alasdair spoke. "Do what you must."

"I'll call with an update soon." Gideon ended the call just as he reached his hotel. He crossed the lobby and took the stairs to his third floor room.

He'd find Rhianna Howell and get the journal.

AN HOUR LATER Gideon sat in a coffee shop across from Rhianna's apartment building, waiting for the female to make an appearance. He'd give her twenty minutes. Then he was going in. Gideon hated waiting, especially after becoming a vampire. As a human, his life was dedicated to the church and to God's will. Although after his attack, and then transformation into a vampire, his patience grew thin. He no longer clung to prayer for guidance. No, he learned if he needed something done, he was better off doing it himself.

A brown-haired female exited the building and stopped at the curb, facing his direction. Gideon focused in, making sure it was her. She had a knee-length coat on and a large bag hanging on her shoulder.

When she entered the coffee shop, he froze, unable to take his eyes off her. The scent of roses filled the air —intoxicating. Breathing in her scent, he groaned and rose from his seat to stand in line behind her. The urge to touch her was too powerful. He didn't even try to stop himself from reaching out to brush his fingers against the ends of her hair.

Fuck. He was acting like a stalker. What the hell?

As if sensing his touch, she turned to face him and frowned. Her eyes flashed with recognition before she turned away. Ah, she knew he was a vampire. *Good.* Although his race had rules of secrecy and enforced them, there were exceptions to the law. Many vampire lords liked to feed from the source. Inhaling, he bit back an unexpected growl. Her natural rose scent was laced with Julian's. She had been with the lord recently.

Leaning in, he whispered so only she could hear him. "I believe you have something of mine."

Spine straightening, she lifted her chin and gave her order to the barista. "Café mocha, please."

Gideon's cock hardened at the sound of her voice. *Damn.* There was only one other time he'd had this reaction to someone. He recognized the mating pull. It had been the same with Alasdair. Could she be their third?

When she moved to the end of the bar, he followed. "I know you have the book."

She met his gaze. "I don't know what you are talking about."

Liar, liar. "Come now, you knew what I am, and that means you are either playing for my team or the other losers."

Her lips twitched. "True, but I could have my own agenda."

The barista placed Rhianna's latte on the counter. "Have dinner with me."

Rhianna narrowed her eyes at him. He couldn't tell if she felt the pull of the mating. Most humans didn't recognize it. Then again, she didn't seem all that human to him. Yet, he couldn't put a finger on what she was.

Finally, she let out a breath. "I'm in the penthouse. Be there at seven." She picked up her coffee and stormed out of the café.

The corner of Gideon's mouth lifted as he watched her ass sway. Nothing was ever easy. But for once, he liked the path the Fates had placed him on. He'd not only found Annamarie's journal, but his and Alasdair's mate as well.

Chapter 4

"WHAT COULD SHE want with it?" asked Alasdair as he sat back in his leather chair, absently tapping his index finger on his desk. His mind whirled with possibilities on why the human female wanted the book. All of which weren't good.

"I'm not sure." Gideon's annoyed voice flowed from the speakerphone.

"She can't keep it," Alasdair growled, turning his chair to glance out the large bay window. The wind blew through the small palms.

"Yes, I know." Gideon sighed. Alasdair could almost see the male running his fingers through his hair. "I'm having dinner with her tonight. I'll snatch the journal the first chance I get."

Even over the phone, Alasdair picked up on the slight hesitation in his lover's speech. "What are you not telling me?"

There was a long silence before Gideon finally let out a breath. "She may be the female we've been looking for."

Alastair stilled. A spark of excitement rose up, but he pushed it down. He would not get his hopes up. Too many times they had thought they found her only to be heart broken when they discovered they were wrong. "You don't have long there. Two more days. Can you get close enough to find out for sure?"

"I believe so. I spoke to her briefly a little while ago and she was bothered by my presence. She also knows I'm a vampire and is annoyed by it." Gideon laughed. "I never had so much fun teasing anyone else but you before."

"Watch it, lover, I might get jealous," he teased. Alasdair was about to speak again but a light knock sounded on the study door. "Come in."

The door opened and Rayne Kensington, the queen's only daughter, entered dressed in a black business suit with a large tote over her shoulder. "Have I come at a bad time?"

"Is that Rayne?" Gideon asked, his voice carrying from the speaker.

Rayne's lips lifted in a smile. "Hello, Gideon. How's the weather in New York?"

"Fucking cold."

She laughed and sat in a chair across from Alasdair. "Better you than me."

"Yeah, yeah. I'll be sure to give Julian your love when I see him."

Rayne's spine went straight, her smile fading. "Good bye, Gideon." She pushed the off button on the speakerphone, ending the call.

Alasdair hid his smile. "Why did you hang up on my mate?"

"I'm not here to discuss Julian."

"The lord is your betrothed." Alasdair raised a brow in challenge.

"That is my business and I'll deal with the lord of New York on my own time."

The laugh burst out before he could contain it. "No wonder he was grumpy when I spoke to him yesterday. Why do you torture him so?"

She rolled her eyes. Pulling a folder from her bag, she set it on the desk. "He likes the chase. Now, if you would sign the treaty, I can return home before morning."

Shaking his head, he skimmed over the document even though he already knew what it entailed. He'd already verbally agreed to it six months prior. But the signature on the magically enhanced parchment bound him to it permanently. If for whatever reason he broke the treaty, he would be killed and his coven would go to one of Lilith's biological children until another lord was chosen to rule it.

After signing the document, he pushed it toward Rayne. "Please give your mother my love."

Rayne nodded, her features softening. "I will. Thank you for this."

"Anytime, Princess."

She let out a low growl before standing and leaving the study, making him laugh.

The pleasure from teasing Rayne died as the room filled with silence. God, he missed Gideon. Missed how he sat on the sofa to his right playing a video game or typing away at his computer. The silence in the study clawed at him, putting him on edge. His skin itched. He needed something to do. Rising from his desk, he headed to his bedroom to change. A run on the beach would help.

With Gideon in his life, there was no room for silence or loneliness. Before the male came into his life a little more than two hundred years ago, Alasdair used to crave the silence. Now, Alasdair preferred the noise, the constant activity that helped passed the days. Because being long-lived was lonely without someone to share it with.

GIDEON HOVERED HIS thumb over his cell phone screen, tempted to call Alasdair back and tease Rayne some more. Although she was like the sister he never had, irritating her would have to wait. He had a woman to visit.

He exited his hotel and shivered as he pulled his leather coat tighter. It was ironic. He couldn't die from the cold, or anything besides having his heart ripped out or his head cut off. Yet the cold still felt like it did when he was human. He hated it then and still hated it now.

The streets of New York were lit up from the multi-colored Christmas lights and decorations in store windows. Many had soft holiday music playing inside that his sensitive hearing picked up on as he passed. It seemed like three lifetimes since he enjoyed the human traditions of their faiths. Christmas use to be his favorite holiday, but he hadn't felt it right to carry his Christian beliefs into his life as a vampire. After all, he was technically classified as a demon.

Turning left, he advanced down the icy sidewalk toward Rhianna's apartment. It was early evening, a few minutes past 6:00. Cars honked in the distance and shoppers bustled around him as they zipped in and out of stores to grab those last minute sales. Gideon clenched his jaw. He sensed the eyes of the city's gargoyles upon him.

Sentries as they were called. Guardians of the night. Each vampire lord had a family or two working and living within their coven. Julian had the largest fleet of the winged beasts because the vampire lord oversaw the security and enforcement of the race.

Footsteps closed in from behind him, and he held in a growl. No need to piss off the female gargoyle. He'd scented her when he passed the last alley. Continuing down the sidewalk, he didn't bother to look over his shoulder.

"Hello, Bless."

She chuckled and by the sound of her boots clicking on the sidewalk, she increased her steps. "Good evening, Gideon. Julian said you'd be in town."

"Only for a few days."

"Oh good. I have other things to do."

Like terrorize small children and grown men. "Don't let me keep you from them then."

She slowed her pace when she reached his side—too close for comfort. Her blonde hair blew in the breeze. A few strands slapped against his arm. Spearing a glance at her, he curled his lip. Her high-heel boots put her about an inch shorter than his six-feet two-inches. She wore tight black jeans tucked inside her boots, and a form-fitting black sweater, a complete contrast of her white-blonde hair. He suppressed a growl for her to back the fuck off. *Focus. Just grab the female, the journal, and go home. Don't start shit with the bitchy gargoyle.*

"But you're fascinating and we have fun when you come to visit. Julian wishes to have dinner with you tomorrow." Her tone had a ring of annoyance to it.

Good. "I will have to decline," he said. "I'm hoping to be on a plane home in the morning."

"Oh, so sad," She lied. The scent of cinnamon apples intensified, slightly indicating she was glad he was leaving so soon. "I'll let my lord know."

He didn't reply, hoping she would leave already. After a few more feet, she stopped and grabbed his arm. When he snarled at her, the flutter of wings sounded from above. Her brother no doubt.

"Let go of my arm, female."

"Listen, vampire. You can't take her from this city without Julian's consent."

He ground his teeth together. "Who are you talking about?"

Bless grinned, showing her sharp fangs. "Don't toy with me. We may be cast in stone during the day, but that doesn't mean we can't hear and see everything. You've been warned, vampire."

In a flash of black she shifted into her winged creature-self and flew off. Gideon ran a hand through his hair while blowing out a breath. He hated gargoyles. Even Alasdair's sentries knew to stay away from him.

Pushing away his irritation, he continued to Rhianna's apartment building. He'd get Julian's permission. However, he didn't need the damned stoned sentry to tell him he had to. *Fucking bitch.*

When he reached the apartment building, he pressed the call button and waited. A buzz came a moment later, indicating he could enter the building.

Rhianna stood beside the elevators, a frown on her face.

Gideon smiled at her. "Good evening."

"That's one opinion."

Her snarky comeback made him laugh. "You could just give me what I want and I'd leave."

She rolled her eyes and entered the elevator. "We'll talk in my apartment out of gargoyle earshot."

Good point. He studied her profile as they rode to the penthouse. Her nose tilted up slightly and her lips weren't too small or too big. Perfect for kissing. His gaze lingered on her mouth until his gums itched, indicating his fangs were about to lower. Tearing his gaze from her, he silently cursed and ground his molars together.

A moment later, the doors swooshed open and she led him into her apartment. Inside was inviting in a warm, elegant way. Cream-colored carpet stretched through the large open living room. The wall across from the main entrance was tinted glass, providing a beautiful view of the city. There was no window dressing. He smiled, realizing that he too would have done the same thing. Why cover up the view?

"Have a seat, please." She disappeared into the next room, which he assumed was the kitchen.

Glancing toward the black, leather sofa, he noticed the journal on the glass coffee table. A grin lifted his lips as he walked over and bent to pick it up. His fingers touched the leather binding and a shock of electricity shot through him, making him stumble backward.

Shit. What the hell was that?

"I figured you couldn't resist."

He jerked his gaze to her and scowled. "What the hell did you do to it?"

She folded her arms. "Why do you want to book?"

Ha. It was the same question he wanted to ask her. Instead, he asked, "Do you know what that book is?"

"A piece of history. Something that needs to be protected and hidden."

Ah. "Hidden from whom?" He took another step toward her. She tensed but didn't move away.

"From those who wish to destroy it."

He closed the distance until they were within a fraction of an inch from each other. Wrapping an arm around her waist, he flattened her body to his. He fought off a groan from the current of pleasure rolling over him, and crushed his mouth to hers, unable to fight the desire any longer. She pressed her palms to his chest and pushed, but when he licked the seam of her lips she opened, allowing him entrance. Fisting his hands into her hair he pulled, drawing a moan from her, and nicked her tongue with his fang. Her rich, rose-scented blood dropped on his tongue just enough for him to taste her.

Instantly, he released her and backed away with a hiss. Anger rose within him. How could he not have known? He paced the living room, pulling at his hair, trying to think. "Why do you smell and look like a human?"

His upset didn't faze her. When he glanced back, she stood with her arms folded and one bare foot tapped rapidly against the floor. "Why do you look human?"

With a snarl, he racked a hand through his hair. "You know what I meant, gargoyle. You hide your aura. Care to tell me how and why?"

"Why should I answer? I'm under Julian's protection."

Gideon laughed. "Why do you not live in the coven?"

"I choose to live here."

He narrowed his gaze. "You're lying."

"You need to leave."

"Is that why there's a gargoyle over your terrace?" He'd heard the creature land a few moments before touching the book.

Irritation colored her cheeks. She stormed to the balcony and opened the doors before yelling, "Sentries have no business here."

A screech sounded just as the flap of wings echoed off the building across from them. Rhianna turned to him, her eyes narrowing. "What do you want with the book?"

"It belongs to my par...my lord. It's a family heirloom, therefore, it belongs to him."

She paused, glanced at the book, and then to him. "How do I know I can trust you?"

"Return to Florida with me and he can prove it to you." He hoped she said yes, because despite the fact she was part gargoyle—and apparently was not affected by the sunlight—she *was* his and Alasdair's mate. He'd never be able to leave her knowing that. Alasdair would kick his ass up and down Destin's beaches for leaving her behind.

She raised her brows. "There is a trust thing."

"Do you trust Julian?"

"I trust he would tell me the truth whether I wanted him to or not." She crinkled up her nose. He realized she didn't trust anyone. Was that the reason she lived in the penthouse alone?

Dropping his guard, he did something he never did around anyone but Alasdair, he revealed his power by picking the book up with his mind. As soon as he did, he cried out and crumbled to the floor. His brain felt like it was on fire, or being fried from the inside out.

Rhianna let out a soft curse and ran to him. She stroked his hair and instantly the pain resigned its hold on him.

Taking slow, deep breaths, he raised his gaze to hers. "What. The hell. Was that?"

She frowned. "I spelled the book when I got it in my possession. If it contains what I believe it does, then it could be used as a weapon in the wrong hands."

No shit. That was why he was there. "What do you believe it holds?"

She hesitated to answer.

If he weren't wiped out by the brain-fry, he'd grab her and the book, and haul them both to Florida tonight.

She sat on the floor beside him. "The notes from one of the first humans to be turned by Lilith."

Well, fuck me.

Chapter 5

"AM I RIGHT?"

Gideon avoided answering her question by pushing himself to stand and wobbling to the door. A small part of Rhianna felt bad, but it was his own fault for using his telekinesis on a spelled book. Couldn't he sense the magic surrounding the thing?

Finally he faced her. His blue depths boring into her, untrusting. "Answer my questions first. Why do you care if the book—assuming you're right—should be hidden?"

It was her turn to look away. She didn't know him or his lord. Not really. For all she knew *they* could be the "wrong hands". Picking up the book, she glanced at him. He was watching her every move. "It's complicated and a long story. Besides I don't know who your lord is."

"Alasdair Morgan."

She knew that, but didn't want Gideon to know she did. "What was his great grandmother's name?"

"Annamarie Morgan. She was born in 3116 BC."

Okay. She could get that information with enough digging and the right keywords. When she didn't speak right away, he added. "The first entry in the book was written in March 1502. She describes a demon attack on her home when she was sixteen."

Carefully, she opened the fragile leather cover and read the first page. He was right. Annamarie had just turned sixteen two months before the attack. Glancing back at the handwriting, Rhianna skimmed the next few paragraphs before she closed the book, and lifted her gaze to Gideon.

His dark blond hair stood on ends as if he constantly pulled at it. Weariness clouded his features, and she wondered if the spell affected him worse than she initially thought. *Oh hell.* Why was she being so stubborn? Crossing the living room, she grabbed his hand. Ignoring the strange tingling sensation that traveled up her arm, she led him to the sofa and pushed him to sit.

"Stay there. I'll make you some tea that will help you feel better."

He shook his head. "I don't want any."

She clicked her tongue and paced to the kitchen. Once there, she put on the kettle. *Stubborn man.* No wait, he wasn't a man, but a vampire. She'd known immediately when he came up behind her at the coffee shop. *The messes you get yourself into, Rhianna.*

Three minutes later she returned to sofa, handed him his tea, and then sat in the chair across from him. "I believe there may be information in the journal that could give the demons a one up in the pending war."

"What do you mean?" he asked.

"Secrets about Lilith that only her lords, or those who were there during the rise of the vampire race would know. Secrets the humans are not ready to know."

His expression didn't change until he sniffed the tea, then his nose crinkled. "What the hell is in here?"

"Chamomile, mint, and ginger. It will help you feel better." She watched him take another sniff before sipping. He was handsome. If she hadn't grown up among vampires, his allure and sexy smile would have trapped her like prey —one of the many talents vampires had to lure humans in and allow them to feed.

Taking a breath and shaking off the odd desire to touch him, she continued. "Annamarie was one of the first humans turned as well as Julian's grandparents. I was aiding him in the search for another artifact when I ran across this journal."

According to her father, there were seven artifacts scattered around the world in order to keep them from Violet, Lilith's sister, queen of the earth-bound demons. Violet tried to expose the vampire race to humans about eight hundred years prior. Instead she only succeeded in placing fear in humans' mind that vampires and demons existed, but Lilith worked with a few loyal humans to discredit everything Violet revealed.

Gideon stared, his features finally relaxing a little. Rhianna knew it wasn't from the tea. She hadn't enchanted it. "Julian sent you to find the artifact," he said.

Of course not. Her father was beyond overprotective when it came to her involvement in the war.

When she didn't reply, Gideon let out a low chuckle. "I thought not. Does he know you have the journal?"

"No. And I don't intend to tell him."

His sinful smile returned. "Well, he knows now thanks to Bless and the other sentries."

Frustration drew a growl from her. "No. Thanks to you, they never paid much attention to me before you showed up."

"Why do you care?" he asked after a brief silence.

"Care about what?"

A brow lifted, but his smile stayed as he spoke. "Whether the demons expose the vampires to humans."

She blew out a breath. Her father said he'd known Gideon since the vampire was turned. If her father trusted him, shouldn't she? *Lilith, help me.*

"I was dropped off on Julian's door step as an infant. He raised me as his own. Taught me everything I know about my powers, and how to survive. In a way, the vampires are as much as my family as the gargoyles and witches are."

Gideon paused with the teacup to his lips and stared as if at a loss for words. After taking a sip and lowering the cup, he asked, "Julian is your father?"

"Not biologically."

"But he raised you. He's your father." He opened his mouth as if to add something but closed it. There was a long pause. "Is that why Bless is protective over you and why gargoyles perch on your roof?"

"Pretty much. I've lived as a human since I was twenty. I don't fit in at the coven, and I was miserable there." She watched his gaze fix on her, not judging but curious. The blond-haired, blue-eyed vampire unnerved her in a way no one else had... ever. She couldn't put her finger on why.

"You don't know who your parents are?"

"No. I'm mostly witch with about a quarter gargoyle. There are also traces of human DNA in me, but I guess we all have that." The truth was, she never cared to know who her parents were. Julian and Bless took good care of her. She'd never wanted for anything.

Standing, she moved to the wall of windows overlooking the terrace and gazed out to the city below her. Silence enveloped her and she breathed it in the night air. The one good thing about vampires was they were quiet even though they gave her headaches — literally. She'd never understood why, but she'd developed some kind of allergy to their scent.

Yet, Gideon didn't have that effect on her.

His reflection in the glass appeared behind hers, making her heartbeat increase and her body warm.

"Why do you not live in the coven where you can be protected?"

She whirled, pinning him with a glare, annoyance hot in her veins. "I don't need protecting."

His pupils narrowed as his fangs peeked from under his top lip. If he was trying to intimidate her, he needed to try a hell of a lot harder. Closing the tiny space between them, he caressed her cheek, sending a wildfire of desire straight to her core. Damned vampire.

His lips twitched as he inhaled, most likely scenting her arousal.

"Answer the question."

Allowing the gargoyle within to rise, she pressed her palm to his chest, feeling his heart beat under the black cotton T-shirt. "I'm a gargoyle with a sorceress's power running in my blood, but you should know that from tasting it earlier. You were too appalled by the taste of gargoyle to notice the magic."

She pushed him hard enough he stumbled backwards. This was bullshit. Why the hell was she talking to the stubborn-ass vampire? She should've thrown him over the balcony when he first opened the French doors.

"I don't have time for this shit. I won't talk to someone who hates me for what I am. Leave."

He glanced at the journal, and then bored his demonic gaze on her. "I'm not leaving without the book."

"The book doesn't leave my sight."

His sensual mouth lifted into a knee-weakening smile. "Then I guess you're coming with me." Too fast for her to track and before he finished speaking, he was at her side wrapping his arms around her.

She stifled a groan as he pressed his lips to her ear and spoke. "I don't hate you. I distrust gargoyles. Don't take it personally, I could never dislike my mate."

Her heart stuttered. *His mate?* Not possible. "I'm not your mate."

"Oh, yes you are. I've never been attracted to a female like I am to you. We've searched for you for a long time. I'm not letting you go so easily." He grounded his erection against her hip and she moaned as a fiery need took over her brain.

"What? We?"

"Alas and I. You are the female meant to complete our mating. It is what's fated."

Complete our mating... What the hell? She squirmed, only making the pleasure within build. By his sharp intakes of breath, she guessed Gideon felt the same way. *Mates? No.*

"I can't. I won't." Old heartache returned, but she pushed it away as she closed her eyes and called her inner gargoyle. "Let me go, please."

"Not until you agree to come to Florida with me and meet Alas. Give us a week and if we can't woo you by then, we'll let you return home." The plea in his tone was completely different from the edginess in it a few moments ago.

Confused by his shift in mood, she shook her head. "Why me?"

He loosened his hold and ran a hand up her arm to her cheek. "Surely Julian had explained mating to you. But in case you need a refresh, vampires can only truly bond with a fated mate. Sure they can mate, but without the bond it's empty. No matter how much the couple works at it, the void can't be filled."

Yes, Julian had explained mating to her. She'd never taken any of it seriously, because she wasn't a vampire. It wasn't until Bless found out about Rhianna's marriage to a human, that the gargoyle warned her not to get attached. Telling her that when a gargoyle falls in love it's forever, and unbearable when that love is lost.

A year later Rhianna caught her husband with his assistant.

The pain from the betrayal nearly drove her insane. She closed herself off to everyone, including Julian. Of course she realized what she felt was rage, and not a broken heart —the gargoyle inside her had not chosen to love her human husband.

"I'm not a vampire. I don't have a fated mate." She stepped out of his embrace, but didn't turn to look at him.

"That is why I ask you to give us a week. Allow the gargoyle and the woman to make the choice together." He held out his hand, palm up.

She didn't take it. "You hate gargoyles."

"I have issues with them, yes. But you're not full-blooded."

She pursed her lips and silently counted to make sure her filter caught the words she couldn't take back once said. "It does matter. The gargoyles are my family as much as Julian is. You have to accept that half of me."

"Then you won't be the only one adjusting during that week."

Adjusting? He seriously had control issues. "I haven't agreed to go."

He gently gripped her arms, and turned her to face him. His smile was genuine, and a little sad. "But you will. I can smell your hesitation and curiosity."

Damn vampire and his ability to scent emotions. "I'll have to gather some things and let my father know I'll be leaving."

"I'll see you in the morning, then." He closed the gap and pressed his lips to hers in an unapologetic, yet seductive kiss. Raw energy exploded within her, spreading heat throughout her body. She groaned and leaned into the kiss, deepening it. Much too soon, he broke contact, his eyes heavy and glowed with arousal. Then he left the penthouse.

Rhianna, you've got to be out of your mind for agreeing to this. Two mates? Yep, she was going insane.

Chapter 6

"SHE'S A GARGOYLE."

Alas chuckled at his lover's growled complaint. "She's only part gargoyle. I spoke to Julian last night after I got off the phone with you, and I do have to warn you that he's not happy about this at all."

Gideon snorted. "I can only imagine. She's his daughter."

How had Julian kept her a secret for as long as he did? It made Alasdair wonder just how powerful Rhianna was. Her witch and gargoyle blood gave her an advantage no vampire or their gargoyle sentries possessed. She could walk in the daylight, unlike her gargoyle kin, and shift on command. The magic coursing through her veins made her stronger than any vampire lord.

"She's a rare female. If the demons knew about her abilities, they'd come after her," Alasdair reminded Gideon. "Are you sure she's the right one?"

A low growl sounded over the wireless connection. "I'm sure. It's the only reason I'm bringing her home."

"The only reason?"

Gideon fell silent for a few moments before replying. "She's like a drug, alluring and beautiful. I can't even be angry at the gargoyle within her."

"Not all of the guardians are like Paris. She was cruel, and mad beyond the point of no return. Sabre should have put her down long before she met you. I regret not going to Lilith about it." Sabre—the vampire lord of the Pacific Northwest—had refused to believe one of his gargoyles had gone mad. Alasdair's heart ached at the memory. He'd found Gideon on the edge of death and the female gargoyle standing over his body with his blood on her hands and mouth.

"My lord, it was not your fault."

Taking a deep breath, Alasdair pushed away the pained memories. His partner was right. "And it isn't Rhianna's fault for being born part gargoyle."

"I know." The reply came out soft, sending a sliver of relief through Alasdair.

Renewed hope that they had finally found the woman who plagued his dreams for so long resurfaced. "Julian has agreed to allow Rhianna to make this decision on her own, no matter what he says in your meeting this morning."

A soft chuckle filtered through the phone. "Julian isn't our biggest challenge. Rhianna is. I think the only reason she agreed to come and stay the week is to make sure the book truly belongs to you."

"Don't worry about her insecurities over the mating, my dear. We will woo her, if she is the one from my visions." Seducing her could be challenging, but Alasdair was a master at getting what he wanted.

"I'm sure she is." Gideon cleared his throat and changed the subject. "How did the meeting go with Rayne?"

"Well. I signed the treaty just as I agreed to with Lilith. The princess wasn't in the mood for small talk." Not that she ever was. Rayne made it a mission to make everyone believe she was a cold-hearted bitch, but Alasdair knew better. She cared for her raced and would do anything to protect them.

Gideon fell silent again and Alasdair sighed. "Gideon, go to your meeting so you can return to me sooner."

"I'll see you soon."

"I'll be waiting." Alasdair paused briefly before adding, "Thank you."

"For what?"

"For believing in me, and finding our mate."

Gideon let out a breath. "I love you, my lord. There is nothing I wouldn't do for you."

Alasdair's heart swelled with a happiness only a select few of his race got a chance to feel in their long, lonely lives. "I love you, too."

He ended the call and sat back in his high-back leather chair. *Please let Rhianna be the one.*

GIDEON SWALLOWED A lump in his throat as he shoved his phone in his pocket. *Damn it.* Two days away from Alasdair and he was already emotional.

"Was that Alasdair?"

He turned to Rhianna, his breath catching as he took her in. Her chestnut hair was damp from the shower, and her brown eyes appeared a little more gold in the morning light. She wore a pair of loose faded blue jeans, and a lavender cashmere sweater that looked amazing against her creamy skin tone.

"Yes. He is eager to meet you."

She averted her gaze. "Oh."

Please don't let her have second thoughts. If she backed out now, there was no stopping Alasdair from coming after her. "Are you okay?"

She shrugged. "I haven't gone to my father's house in about a year."

Narrowing his gaze, he crossed his arms over his chest. "Why not?"

"Because...I married a human without Julian's consent."

Stepping closer to her, Gideon reached out to brush his knuckles down her cheek. "Is that why you live here instead of the coven?"

She nodded. "I couldn't face them with my failures."

The thought of her with another man beside Alasdair sent a river of lava through his veins. She was theirs. No one had a right to claim her, and they especially didn't have the right to hurt her.

"Why did you divorce?"

Facing him, she scanned his face, eye narrowed. "I caught him fucking his assistant."

One side of his mouth lifted. "Do you kiss your father with that mouth?"

Instantly she relaxed and smiled. "Yes, I do."

He wrapped an arm around her waist, and drew her closer so their bodies meshed together. Need burned through him, hardening his cock. "Every moment I'm around you, the need to possess you grows stronger. As does the desire to be inside you with my fangs and cock."

She groaned and threaded her fingers into his hair, her nails gently scrapping his scalp. "Do you kiss your partner with that mouth?"

A chuckle escaped. "I do."

Gold swirled in her brown eyes, revealing for the first time her witchy side as she held eye contact with him. "We shouldn't keep my father waiting."

With a low growl he released her, and stepped away. *Fuck.* He couldn't think with her around. What the hell was it going to be like when the three of them bonded? He strode to the door, opened it, and waited for her pass. He just hoped Julian had enough time to absorb the idea of Rhianna leaving town, and mating outside the coven before they got there.

The vampire lord of New York was the poster boy of over-possessive vampire. He would be twenty times worse with his daughter.

Gideon, how do you get yourself into the shit you do?

Chapter 7

A SHIVER SHOT up Rhianna's spine as she entered her father's study. It wasn't from the coming winter storm, but from the less-than-pleased glare of the man behind the large cherry-stained oak desk.

Julian sat tapping a pen slowly against the wood. His navy blue gaze locked with hers as she approached. The sleeves to the white button-down were rolled halfway up his forearms, his usual casual dress.

Moving closer from behind, Gideon's warmth soothed her nerves. *Like a mate should.*

Straightening her spine, she greeted her father with a warm smile. "Good morning, Father." She didn't really need his permission, but it was respectful for her and the vampire she was leaving with to meet with Julian before taking off. *Politics.*

Stepping from behind to her side, Gideon gave a short nod to Julian. "Good morning, my Lord."

Julian raised a blond brow and his lips twisted, easing some of her tension. Motioning to the chair in front of his desk, Julian said, "We've known each other for over two hundred years and not once have you ever greeted me so politely."

Gideon dropped into a chair across from her father and lifted one shoulder. "There's a first for everything."

Rhianna studied one vampire then the other. An odd sense of tension passed between them. Somehow she didn't think it was all about her. Gideon's jaw worked, and he clenched his hands over the armrest.

After a brief moment, Julian relaxed his shoulders and sat back in his chair. "Have you told Rhianna of Alasdair's illness?"

Gideon let out a low growled. "My lord has never been better."

Julian held the male's stare for several moments before glancing to her. A cold sensation sliced through her gut. She was not going to like what her father was about to say.

"Alasdair is one of the oldest vampires known to be alive. He has battled bloodlust for the last century."

Gideon jumped to his feet, slamming his hands on the desk and leaning in closer to Julian.

Rhianna's heart pounded as fear for what her father would do to Gideon lit up every nerve ending. Opening her mind, she allowed her magic to run wild inside her. She would zap both of them if either tried to harm the other.

Another growl rumbled from Gideon, before he spoke. "I said he has a handle on it. Plus we've found our mate to complete the bond."

Julian, unaffected by Gideon's outburst, laid down his pen and picked up an envelope. He handed it to her, ignoring Gideon's anger. "She needs to know what's she's getting into."

"Why are you doing this?" she bit out with her own growl. "It's not like you to spill secrets that aren't yours to tell. Besides, I can take care of myself."

He cut her a narrow-eyed glare and gripped her hand when she reached for the envelope. "Inside this is the contract pledging my alliance to Alasdair's coven. Don't give it to him until you've made your choice to be their mate. Ask the lord what it means to have the illness. Be aware that completing the mating bond doesn't always save a vampire from the madness bloodlust causes."

She snatched her hand from his, taking the contract with it. Fury rose, but she squashed it. No use in angering her father further. She could already tell he didn't like any of this, but it was her life. She would make her own decisions with or without his approval, and he knew that.

"I'm going to discover who I am and who my mates are. Plus it will give me the opportunity to learn more about why the demons want the artifacts. I can help with this war."

A tic formed his Julian's temple. "This war is not your concern."

Gideon whistled. "Now I understand. You allowed her to live as a human to keep her hidden from the demons."

Julian returned his glare to the other vampire. "She was happy."

Rhianna started to shake. *No, she wasn't happy.* She constantly had to mask her magic and her gargoyle strength.

Before she could speak, Gideon rushed on. "You think she was happy hiding? None of her friends know who or what she is. That's no life."

Julian bared his fangs. "She is my daughter and my responsibility."

"He's right," she said, but Julian didn't hear her.

"Rhi, did your *mate* tell you he was a priest before he was attacked by a blood-crazed gargoyle and left for dead? That Alasdair found him and saved his life by turning him into a vampire against his will?" Julian held Gideon's stare as he said the words.

She shook her head, trying to process. Confusion, anger, and fear churned inside her. Her father was trying to hurt Gideon. Never in her thirty-five years of life had she witnessed him act this way. If this was his attempt to convince her to stay in New York, it wasn't working. If Alasdair and Gideon were her true mates, she had a right to know —didn't she?

Yes, she did.

A low growl escaped Gideon. She glanced at him and saw he had a death grip on the chair arm. "Why are you doing this?"

Julian's eyes flashed a lighter blue before he snarled, "She has a right to know what she's getting herself into."

"She has the right to discover it on her own."

Julian leaned forward, eye narrowing and the tips of his fangs sticking from under his top lip. "She's my daughter and I say whom she mates."

What? How dare he talk about her like she was a child? Rhianna open her mouth, but didn't have the chance to speak her mind before Gideon flew across the desk and tackled Julian. The vampires rolled and punched each other until she sent a warning shot of power to the floor next to her father's head. They froze, and stared at her.

"Enough! Father, I'm going to Florida." She stormed out of the study, slamming the door behind her.

She shook from the rush of anger that over took her. *Fuck!* She'd never wanted to kill something as bad as she did in that moment. Her boots *clicked* against the hard wood as she rushed through the great room to the front door. She didn't stop until she reached the waiting car her father had arranged to take them to the airport.

Sometimes, being a vampire lord's daughter sucked.

"YOU'VE BEEN TOO quiet." Gideon had watched Rhianna stare out the plane's window since they took off thirty minutes before. She refused to talk to him or look at him, and it was driving him mad.

She let out a sigh and faced him. "Was he right? Is that why you don't like gargoyles?"

"Yes. About everything." He set down the book he was pretending to read. "It was a very long time ago and I was a different man then."

"What happened?"

He shook his head, wishing he could wipe the knowledge from her memories. He didn't want her knowing about his darkest time. Didn't want her to pity him.

"Gargoyles always perched on the church steeple where I served. Although, I didn't know before that night they were living, breathing, shape-shifting creatures."

She made a cute growl-like noise at his comment, but he didn't apologize for calling them creatures. That was what they were, and would always be to him.

Unfastening her seatbelt, she moved to the seat next to his. "You said until that night. What was different?"

"After I exited the church to head home something caught my attention. When I looked up, I noticed a gargoyle I hadn't seen before. But she wasn't in stone like the others perched on the rooftop. She was alive, crouched down with glowing red eyes, and watching me." He closed his eyes, and rested his head against the headrest. The familiar rush of fear and shock he had felt that night swirled in his mind again.

"It happened so fast. At first my human mind didn't understand what I was seeing. The word demon flashed in my mind a split second before she attacked. All the chanting and prayers didn't stop her razor sharp claws from tearing into my chest and feeding on my blood. I must have passed out at some point. Either from blood loss or from the pain, I'm not sure. When I woke two days later, I was in Alasdair's bedroom."

"With fangs." She reached over and laced her fingers with his.

"Yes. I hated him, and never understood why he would curse me. Why didn't he let me die?" Gideon brought her hand to his lips.

"What changed? I mean you're his mate now."

Gideon smiled. "Alas is a charmer. It is better that he tells you our love story. He tells it much better than I."

She fell silent for a long while before speaking again. "My father was wrong."

"About what?"

"The war not concerning me. I'm a witch. Witches have battled with demons since the beginning of time. It's in my blood to take a stand against them." She tightened her grip around his hand. He traced the edge of her thumb with his, trying to calm her.

"I agree with you. Julian only means to protect you. He cares for you deeply."

"I know." She twisted in the seat to face him. "Will everything be okay between him and Alasdair's covens?"

"You mean after that little tiff? Sure. You should see him and Alasdair go at it." Gideon laughed. "They are like brothers. Fighting one minute, sharing war stories the next. Don't worry about it."

When she yawned, he wrapped an arm around her shoulder and drew her in so her head rested on his chest. "Get some sleep, love."

She snuggled into him and closed her eyes. Her rose scent invaded his senses, calming and intoxicating.

There was no doubt in his mind she was their mate, and could be the one to cure Alasdair of his bloodlust.

God, he hoped.

Chapter 8

ALASDAIR PACED THE foyer. Every muscle in his body tensed and his stomach churned with each passing minute. The anxiety clinched him when he woke that morning and had no indication of letting go anytime soon. At least not until Gideon arrived with Rhianna. The downfall of all the anticipation building inside him was that it triggered his bloodlust. He'd hunted that morning, hoping to calm the ever-clawing hunger. Still, he craved more blood.

Fuck. Where the hell are they?

"My Lord?"

Glancing over his shoulder, he met the watchful eye of one of his most loyal sentries, Cassian. The gargoyle had been his great grandmother's guardian since the day Lilith found her in the forest running from demons at the age of sixteen.

"I'm fine. Have you heard from them?" He glanced down at his phone as the sound of a car pulling into the gravel driveway. "Never mind."

He rushed to the door and opened it. Gideon stepped out of the car and Alasdair pulled him into a tight hug, inhaling his scent as well as the scent of the female he'd brought home. For the love of Lilith, it was *her*! Their mate. He knew by her scent.

When the small brunette emerged from the backseat, Alasdair froze, and stared into her golden-brown eyes. She gazed back at him, curiousness flashed in her glaze before she smiled and held out her hand. Ignoring her hand, he pulled her into a hug and buried his nose in her neck. Her body stiffened, but he didn't sense fear. Her rose scent intensified as if she felt the same pull of desire he did.

Good.

Gideon clasped him on the shoulder and squeezed. "We should go inside and get Rhianna settled."

Alasdair pulled back and stared at the female, smiling like an idiot. Her brown hair was pulled back into a ponytail with a few stray strands framing her beautiful, natural face. Yet, there was leeriness in the golden depths of her eyes.

After a moment she stepped back. A nervous laugh slipped from her lips. She followed Gideon inside, and Alasdair ground his teeth as he turned to pace after them.

Closing the door behind him, he demanded, "What's going on?"

Gideon let out a soft curse. "Julian told Rhianna of your *illness*."

"Bastard." Alasdair inhaled a deep breath. "Although, I did expect it."

"It was uncalled for," Rhianna said as she scanned the great room, smiling when her gaze lighted on the painting over the fireplace. "Is that your grandmother?"

"Yes, great grandmother Annamarie, How did you know?" Alasdair stepped closer to her.

Turning to meet his stare, she smiled. "Just a guess." Her golden gaze brightened, showing the magic running in her blood. She lifted a hand as if to touch his face, but much to his disappointment, she lowered it. "You are different than Gideon. Polar opposites. The priest and the vampire."

Alasdair snorted. "I guess my secrets weren't the only ones told."

Rhianna crinkled her nose. "My father wasn't on his best behavior."

"He never is, dear." Alasdair held out his arm to her, and he almost sighed in relief when she took it. "Come, I'll show you to our room."

She jerked to an abrupt stop, tugging her arm from his. When he glanced over his shoulder, he smiled at the way she crossed her arms and pursed her lips.

"What it is?

"I agreed to come here and spend a week with the both of you. To get to acquainted and learn more about the book. I didn't agree to jump into bed with either of you." She glared at him, the gold in her eyes shifting to the crimson of her gargoyle half.

He pivoted to face her and cupped her cheek. She tugged away from his touch. A heavy weight settled in his chest, followed by the urge to reach out and draw her curvy body to his. They'd looked too long for her.

Taking a calming breath, he pushed away his feelings, not wanting her see his weakness.

"You can have your own room." Wrapping a hand around her nape, he pulled her to him. He lowered his lips to her ear, inhaling her intense rose scent mixed with the slight musk of her desire. "I can smell your desire for us. Don't keep us waiting too long. We will chase you."

As he lifted his head, he met Gideon's gaze. The male had passion in his blue eyes, clearly sensing Alasdair's own arousal. With a growl, Alasdair backed away from the female, and continued down the hall, stopping at the bedroom beside the master suite. He opened the door for her, and gave a short nod.

"Please make yourself at home. Anything you need, just ask." Before the impulse to seduce her into submission took over, he fled to the master suite he and Gideon shared. Each step away from them spiked his need. He'd gone too long without release. With Gideon in New York for two days, he regretted not taking what he needed from his lover before the separation. Rhianna's presence now only intensified his desires, making it nearly impossible to think coherently.

He crossed the room, passing the oversized king bed in the middle off the left side of the room. Opening the French doors, he stepped out onto the balcony and inhaled the salty air. His blood sang in his veins, calling out to the female in the next room. Not knowing what to do with his unsteady hands, he braced them on the railing, white knuckling the metal. He scanned the white sand covered beach; mesmerized by the way it sparkled in the setting sun. The roar of the ocean calmed him, but only a little.

Several moments passed before the bedroom door opened, and then clicked shut again. Gideon's rich, rosemary scent reached out to him as the male approached from behind. Alasdair didn't move, even though the other male's arousal swirled around him. He knew full well what Gideon had planned.

Gideon stopped behind him, and the warmth from the male's body enveloped Alasdair, making him grip the railing tighter to keep from touching his mate. Since they became lovers over a hundred years ago, Gideon had always been the dominant one in bed. Alasdair relished in it. As the vampire lord, he always had to be in control. Allowing someone else to take the reins reminded him he had a compassionate side. It also felt damn good to let go.

"Take off your shirt."

Gideon's growl sent a shockwave straight to his dick. Slowly Alasdair released the railing, and tugged his shirt over his head. When Gideon pressed his lips to Alasdair's bare back, he sucked in a sharp breath. Scorching desire burned in his veins. His dick hardened and pressed painfully into the zipper of his jeans.

"Hmm. I've missed the taste of you." Gideon traced a hand up Alasdair's leg. Then slid it around to cup his mate through Alasdair's dress pants. Alasdair's body bucked under Gideon's touch. Gideon kissed his neck before whispering, "Turn around."

He complied and Gideon cupped his head in his hands and kissed him. Alasdair gripped the other vampire's hips and squeezed. Gideon groaned and swiped his tongue inside Alasdair's mouth. Tingles of desire skittered over Alasdair's skin as their mouths moved against each other.

Gideon broke the kiss and nipped his way to Alasdair's throat, then further down until he let go and dropped to his knees. Alasdair clenched the bars to the balcony railing behind him, not daring to touch Gideon. Not yet.

Much too slow, his lover undid the button to Alasdair's jeans, and then lowered the zipper. The denim slid down his legs, allowing the chilled gulf breeze to nip at his skin. The cool air did nothing to ease the heat spreading through Alasdair as Gideon cupped him and rolled his balls in one hand.

"I want your mouth on me." Alasdair panted, trying like hell not to come just yet.

Gideon let out a soft chuckle, and tugged Alasdair's boxer-briefs down next. He wrapped his long fingers around Alasdair's cock, and guided it into his mouth.

Liquid fire rippled through Alasdair as Gideon sucked and licked in slow, deliberate, teasing pulls. Alasdair sank his fingers into Gideon light brown hair, and moved his hips, fucking Gideon's mouth.

A wave of pleasure rolled through him, intensifying with each thrust. Letting his head fall back, Alasdair's body tensed as he tried to control the orgasm from shoving him over the edge. He wanted to ride the pleasure wave just a little longer. But, when Gideon tightened his grip, took him deeper, and dipped his fingers into Alasdair's ass, his climax slammed into him.

Alasdair roared and fisted his hand tighter in his lover's hair, riding out the last shudder.

Gideon stood and Alasdair gazed into his eyes. A sensual, lazy smile lifted his lover's lips. "Did I tell you I missed you?" asked Gideon.

Alasdair cupped his head and kissed him quickly. "You might have mentioned it."

Taking his hand, Gideon tugged him into the room and to the bed. "Get comfortable."

He watched Gideon's ass as the male disappeared into the bathroom. Anticipation warmed him as he climbed on the bed. A moment later Gideon came back with a tube of lube and a small towel.

Desire darkened his blue eyes as he approached. Alasdair fell in love all over again. When he reached out, Gideon gripped his wrist. "Lay back."

The soft-spoken command ignited the spark of desire inside and he did as he was told. He watched the other man remove his clothes. Alasdair's dick filled and he gripped himself, slowly stroking as Gideon eased onto the bed to hover over him. Leaning down, Gideon captured his lips in a deep, sensual kiss, dipping his tongue inside. Alasdair moaned into the kiss. He released his cock and wrapped his hand around Gideon's hard length instead.

Gideon hissed out a grown, and broke the kiss to trail his lips down Alasdair's jaw to his neck where bit down gently, teasingly, not breaking the skin. A jolt of pleasure burned in his veins and Alasdair teetered on the edge, barely able to keep from flipping his lover over and taking him hard and fast.

No, this was Gideon's game. He would get his turn, later.

Lifting his head, Gideon stared at him from above. One corner of his lips tugged slightly. "Someone is impatient."

"Why do you torture me, love. Give me what I want before I lose it."

A chuckle escaped Gideon as he rose to stand on his knees between Alasdair's thighs. With heavy lids, Gideon picked up the lube and squeezed some out onto his fingers before rubbing it over Alasdair's hole. Then he slid a finger inside. Pleasure uncoiled and raced through Alasdair.

Withdrawing his finger a few moments later, Gideon positioned his cock to enter.

Alasdair growled, his impatience growing. Vampires didn't have to worry about diseases, so there was no need for condoms. The only reason Gideon would hesitate would be to tease him.

"Gideon," Alasdair warned.

The male responded by pushing inside, filling him. Tingles skittered over his flesh, intensifying the pleasure with each thrust. Gideon took Alasdair's cock, and stroked in tempo with each thrust, making him dig his heals into the mattress. Alasdair's fangs extended over his lower lip, and he knew his eyes had gone black by the way Gideon's lips twitched. The male lowered his head, his own fangs lengthening. Then Gideon struck, biting the spot where his neck and shoulder met.

The sharp pain followed by pleasure intensified the fiery passion between them. Alasdair cried out, and came at the same time Gideon jerked, sinking into his own release.

Chapter 9

"THE WITCH HAS the book."

Gritting her teeth, Violet fisted her hands and held back from lashing out at her consort. Wyn meant well, but his grasp for the fucking obvious struck her last nerve. "Yes, I'm well aware of the witch's involvement and her intent to keep the journal out of our hands."

Rhianna would have to be dealt with. "Where is she now?"

"She's in Florida with Alasdair. My source tells me she is his mate and he seeks to form a triad." He made a growl-like noise in his throat. "If they complete the bond—"

Violet whirled around, and held a hand up, cutting off his irritating need to tell her shit she already knew. "I'm aware of what would happen. My sister would have a very powerful vampire lord in the south. However, he would only be one, and there are many more of us."

She needed that journal as much as she needed to stop Alasdair from completing the triad bond. A chuckle rumbled from Wyn, making her cut a glare at him. "What's so fucking funny?"

"I had a thought."

Which was dangerous on most occasions, but she didn't comment. Very rarely he came up with some good ideas.

"Alasdair continues to fight his blood lust. What if we upped his dose of the enhancer?"

"Wyn, love, you're a genius." She crossed the room to her desk, and fired up her laptop, something Wyn taught her to use when they hooked up two years ago. "We need a larger group in the south."

If they were able to stop the triad and grab the journal, she would finally have the upper hand in the war against her sister, Lilith, and her precious vampires.

Walking up behind her, Wyn placed his hands on Violet's shoulders, and kneaded her tense muscles. He leaned in and bit her ear lobe.

She groaned as he growled, "I know just how to do that, my Queen."

RHIANNA PACED HER too-quiet room, her gut churning with worry. After Alasdair stormed off, Gideon had helped a young male echo demon—servants to the vampire race—carry in her bags. However, the Gideon hadn't stayed around to answer any questions about Alasdair's sudden shift in mood. Instead, he'd just disappeared, leaving her alone.

She refused to feel bad about turning the vampire lord down. It wasn't her fault he had unrealistic hopes. *Not my problem.*

She dug out her silk gloves from her suitcase, and then retrieved the journal from her tote. After putting the gloves on, she opened the journal. She frowned, and blinked several times. *No, it couldn't have.* The words in the journal had changed during the trip from New York. She couldn't explain it, but the pages were no longer written in English. Plus, the spell she placed on it had vanished, replaced with a darker, older magical signature. Something had activated an ancient spell, superseding hers.

She hovered her hand over the leather cover. The magic felt thick, oily, and gave her goose flesh. She carefully touched the book with a bare finger, closed her eyes, and waited to be knocked on her ass... or worse. When nothing happened, she picked the book up. Tingles of heavy magic kissed her skin, but then receded. It was like the spell—or it could very well be a curse—was testing her, but for what?

Gideon claimed the book belonged to Alasdair's family, and she'd believed him. He'd been able to paraphrase the first page. However, those same words were unreadable now. If the book indeed belonged to the vampire lord, then he would know if it was cursed. Wouldn't he?

She'd hope to avoid the two vampires for the rest of the day so she could think clearly. Being around Gideon for the short time in New York was intense enough, but being around both men had tripled her libido. Damn, if she didn't want to say fuck it and shack up with them now.

No.

She had to clear her mind and focus on the journal.

Gathering her courage, she exited the room, and knocked on the door next to hers. The rustling of sheets made heart hammer in her throat. Oh dear Lilith, they were having sex. Or had just finished? The thought heated her whole body. *Shit.* She found the images of their naked bodies tangled together to be damn hot.

The door opened —Gideon stood before her in nothing but his jeans with the top button undone. She swallowed, and tried to mask the wave of desire crashing over her. It was no use.

His nostrils flared, and his lips curved into a sensual smile. "Did you want to join us?"

"I..." What the hell had she wanted? *Oh yeah, the journal.* "There's something wrong with the book."

Alasdair appeared behind Gideon, and wrapped his arms around the other male's chest and waist. Rhianna couldn't help but admire how beautiful they were together.

A soft chuckle escaped Alasdair, drawing her attention back to his face. "What do you mean?"

She glanced down the hall, then back at them. "Can we take this somewhere more private?"

Alasdair kissed Gideon's neck while holding Rhianna's gaze. Her heartbeat quickened as she saw a hint of fang before the vampire lord disappeared into the bathroom.

Gideon stepped aside and motioned for her to come in.

She glanced to the bathroom again, and could see Alasdair tying the sash of his robe through the crack in the door. She pulled her gaze from the bathroom and walked to the French doors that led out to a large balcony, trying like hell not to stare at the huge unmade bed taking up half the room. "After you two left my room, I pulled the journal out of my bag." Opening the journal, she turned it so he could see the writing. "It was in English at my penthouse. When we arrived here it changed. Plus my protection spell has been removed."

Gideon drew his brews together as he studied the book. "How is that possible?"

She stepped closer to him and shoved the book at him, making him jerk away. "Just hover your hand over it to see it you sense anything."

With a low growl, he slowly raised his hand and inched it closer to the book. "I don't understand. Are you sure you didn't do anything to it?"

Yanking the book away from him, she bit her lower lip to keep the string of curses circling in her mind from escaping. It hurt a little that he'd even think she did something. Okay, so she did spell the journal in New York, but that was to keep anyone but her from accessing the book.

"The journal is cursed." Alasdair's low tone drew her attention to the vampire as he crossed the room to them.

"So I'm not going crazy," she said, offering the book to the vampire lord.

He held his hands up, and shook his head. "I can't touch it in its current state. And no you're not crazy. But I'm not sure why it activated."

Gideon reached over and poked the leather cover with an index finger, sighing when nothing happened to him. He extracted it from her grasp and opened it. "What language is this?"

Alasdair *tssked*. "All languages mixed together to make no sense."

Rhianna studied the diverse groupings of letters, wondering what type of spell had been used, if it was indeed a curse. A curse used dark magic, and usually some kind of sacrifice. Lifting her hand she touched the middle of page and traced a few words before Alasdair grabbed her wrist. Soon after, he hissed out a string of curses while cradling his arm.

Closing the book, and setting it down in a nearby chair, she moved to the lord. "What were you thinking?"

His blue gaze met hers, and he jerked out of her reach. "What were you doing?"

One, two...

"I was seeing if I could tell what type of spell was used."

Gideon shifted beside her. "Do you think whatever changed in the book altered your spell?"

"No. My magic doesn't work on it anymore. Besides my spell was directed at everyone besides me. This one seems to be directed only at Alasdair." She faced him and thought for a minute. "Use you telekinesis on it."

Gideon shook his head. "Hell, fucking no. That shit hurt."

"Poor baby." She picked up the book and sat in the chair beside the balcony doors.

"It's a curse." Alasdair muttered as he sat on the edge of the bed in front of her. His robe fell open just enough she caught view of his inner thigh before averting her gaze.

"How sure are you?"

"About eight hundred years ago Lilith's sister, Violet, stole the journal from Annamarie, and was going to release it to the humans as proof vampires existed." He watched her, his vivid blue eyes darkening.

Somehow she knew it wasn't out of anger, nor was it from desire. Could it be the bloodlust surfacing?

Much too fast for her to track, Alasdair pulled her chair so her knees touched his. Gideon stretched out across the bed behind him, a grin on his face. Her heart pounded and she glanced from one vampire to the other. Alasdair cupped her cheek, drawing her full attention to him. His handsome, strong features captivated her.

Alasdair didn't look a day over thirty-five, but she knew he was much older. Julian said he was one of the oldest living vampires on earth.

"Set the book on the table beside you, please. Its presence is disturbing." When he spoke, she found it hard to tear her gaze from his lips. Suddenly, she wanted to touch them, kiss them.

Nodding, she did as he asked.

Once the book was out of her hand, he sighed and leaned his forehead to hers. "Thank you."

Unclear on what to do, she froze in place. Touching him was soothing in an erotic kind of way, so pulling away wasn't an option. However, she was confused by the emotions building inside her, the connection she felt for both men. She took a deep breath and asked, "Tell me about the curse."

Alasdair's lips lifted in a sensual smile. "Only if you lay between us."

She pulled away and studied him, but before she could verbally protest, he placed a finger over her lips. "No sex. Not yet. Just lie with us."

"You mean cuddle?"

"Yes."

His eyes changed again, and she couldn't help but ask. "Why do your eyes change color? I haven't noticed Gideon's do it or any other vampire I've met." Waiting for an answer, she feared she'd overstepped some kind of personal boundary.

After a long pause, his smile faded. "They change with my emotions, but mostly it's because of my constant fight to control the bloodlust."

Cupping his face in her hands, she kissed him lightly on the lips. "Thank you for being honest with me."

His brilliant smile returned, warming her heart.

Pushing the chair back, she stood and kicked off her shoes before crawling onto the bed. Gideon moved to the side so she was sandwiched between them. Alasdair tugged her closer until her head rested on his chest.

"When my great grandmother discovered the journal missing, she went directly to Lilith. At that time there were no lords, and the vampire race was small enough they lived together in one region." Alasdair lifted a strand of her hair and twirled it in his fingers.

Gideon rubbed her arms in circular motions.

"What did Lilith do?" She snuggled into them a little more, relaxing in a way she never had with anyone.

"She contacted a local witch and pledged an alliance with her. The catch was the witch had to steal the journal back, place a curse on it, and hide it, along with the five other artifacts." He pressed his lips to her head and she sighed.

They *were* her mates. She sensed it in every caress. Could she truly relax and stop running from the fear of another heartache? She wasn't sure, not yet.

Gideon rose up on one arm, and nipped at her shoulder. "I'm starved. Why don't we clean up and go out?"

"That sounds great." Alasdair said just as Rhianna's stomach growled.

She laughed. "I was going to say that I was comfortable, but I guess my belly has outed me."

"Good." Alasdair kissed her forehead and patted her bottom, startling her. "We'll meet downstairs in fifteen minutes."

She scrambled out of their bed, grabbed the book, and headed for the door. When she reached it, Alasdair called her name.

"Yes?" she asked, pausing at the door.

"Can you break the curse?"

"Once I figure out how it was done, yes."

The vampire lord smiled again, and this time it reached his eyes. "Thank you."

A sense of purpose mixed with excitement filled her. She nodded, and darted from the room. Somehow she would break the curse. She would start searching for answers right after her date with two gorgeous vampires.

Chapter 10

"HOW DO I LOOK?"

Gideon laughed at the way Alasdair tugged the sleeves of his light blue dress shirt. "You are as handsome as ever." He stepped up behind the vampire and rested his chin on Alasdair's shoulder. "She's coming around."

Alasdair gave a short nod. "Yes. She feels the pull, but she's still afraid to get to close."

"It's the gargoyle in her that is hesitating. She was married to a human for several years and grew to care for him. Then he betrayed her, broke her heart." Gideon tried to keep the anger from his tone, but failed.

"We won't hurt her." Alasdair sounded equally bothered by the mention of the loser-ass-human. Gideon would have to find the asshat and pay him a little visit.

The smell of roses drifted from the stairs, drawing both his and Alasdair's attention to the dark-haired beauty descending them. She wore a white thigh-length sweater, and black tight-fitting jeans tucked inside knee-hi boots.

"Good, God, have mercy," Gideon whispered.

"Hold your tongue, love. You aren't a priest anymore."

A laugh burst free as Gideon elbowed his partner in the side and addressed Rhianna, "You look beautiful."

Her cheeks colored. "I wasn't sure what to wear."

Alasdair stepped forward and offered her a hand. She took it without hesitation.

Gideon's heart warmed at the sight of her and Alasdair. They were beautiful together. Every nerve ending lit up when she smiled at both of them.

She reached out to cup Alasdair's face. "I'm not sure of a lot of things right now, but Bless always told me to follow my intuition. And I don't have to tell you that Gargoyles mate for life, just like vampires."

Gideon wrapped an arm around her and kissed her neck. "We'll be gentle with your heart."

"Good." She winked at him and looped her other arm with his. "Now where are you taking me for dinner?"

DINNER WAS FABULOUS and the view of the sun setting over the gulf was beautiful. They'd taken her to a small Oceanside restaurant within a ten-minute walk down the beach from the house. The weather was cool enough to be comfortable, but not too cold. She could get use to life on the beach. However, it was odd to be in such a warm temperatures two days before Christmas.

After eating, they strolled down the beach without their shoes through the cool sand. The full moon hung overhead like a beacon lighting their way home.

"It's so pretty here."

Gideon linked his fingers with hers. "I couldn't imagine living anywhere else."

She glanced to Alasdair, who'd gone quiet in the last few minutes. "What about you?"

He gave her a forced smile, and then resumed scanning the beach. "I've lived here all my life. The beach house belonged to my parents."

"Really?" She hesitated, unsure how to ask her next question. "Are they...?"

Alasdair smiled. "My parents are alive. My father stepped down from being the lord of the southeastern region right after the artifacts were hidden. He and my mother live with Lilith in St. Augustine."

Pulling her gaze to his, she didn't stop the shock from showing on her face. "The queen lives that close?"

Gideon linked his fingers with hers. "Lilith has many homes all over the US. She moves around to keep her sister from finding her."

That made sense. The queen's security was the most important.

When she opened her mouth to speak, an icy chill went up her spine. The hairs on her nape rose. She tightened her grip on Gideon's hand. "What is that?"

"Demons," Gideon hissed.

As if saying the word summoned the hell spawns, two demons materialized a few feet in front them. One looked human, with hair that appeared silver in the moonlight. The other had a bluish hue to his skin tone, or at least it looked that way under the moon, and two small horns sticking out of his forehead.

Both vampires stepped in front of her, blocking her from the demons. She gritted her teeth and fisted her hands. All her life she'd been protected and guarded like a helpless child. Well she was far from helpless. Plus, Bless had trained her to fight since she the age of four —her first shift to gargoyle form.

When the demons charged, she opened up herself to her magic, allowing it flow through her veins, ready for her command. Her gargoyle paced, waiting to be let out. *Not yet.* She took a few steps back to get a clear shot at the demons without harming her mates. Taking another step away from the fight, she froze when clawed hands wrapped around her arms. The stench of sulfur made her nose tingle.

Damn demons.

She reached back, gripped the demon by the head, and let go of her magic. The warm flow of energy shot into the creature's skull, making him cry out and release her. Whirling around, she noted four other demons running toward them. *Fuck.*

"More incoming!"

With nothing more than a thought, she released the hold on her beast. Her body shook as the gargoyle rose to the surface, and let out a roar. In a flash of black and silver she shifted, her wings extending, lifting her from the ground. From the air she had clearer aim. She conjured a fire spell and thrust it at the closest two hell spawns. It hit them with quick efficiency. They screamed as the fire consumed them.

One of the two remaining ones shifted into a winged hellhound, and flew at her. *Damn it.* She turned and darted through the air, throwing fireballs as she went. But it evaded every single one.

Okay, think, Rhianna.

She had an issue with aiming while flying. Bless had said it was her gargoyle blocking her witch sight. *That was it! Sight.* He couldn't catch her if he couldn't see her.

"Invisible I'll be." Her aura shimmered to an iridescent glow, hiding her from view.

She flew straight up several feet.

The demon continued his track, then stopped to hover in mid-air, searching the area.

Ha! She dove, hitting him like a linebacker with a shoulder to his gut. They tumbled through the air before hitting the ground. The impact made her lose concentration on her cloaking spell. Rolling to her feet about a yard from him, she focused on his body language.

The demon snarled and rushed toward her. She darted out of the way, but not fast enough. His claw sliced across her upper arm, making her cry out.

She spun around and snarled. "Bastard."

An unexpected hit from behind knocked her to the ground. Trying to catch her breath, she reached back with her claws and pierced the thigh of the demon pinning her to the ground.

He roared out in pain. Then with a quick *snap* the asshole broke her wing.

A scream ripped from her throat as pain seared through her wing, to her back, and spread through her whole body like she was on fire. Tears blurred her vision and it was hard to think and breathe through the pain.

Suddenly the demon's weight was yanked off her and Alasdair face appeared in her line of sight. His dark brows knitted together, and his forehead creased.

"Shh. Don't move and don't shift." He smoothed her hair from her face. "Sorry, love. We have to move you to the house."

She nodded, and braced herself.

Gideon knelt down on her other side, and gently wrapped his hands around her arm. She wished she could turn her head to see him. Instead she lifted her gaze to Alasdair, and laid her cheek against the cool sand. "I'm ready."

Together the vampires lifted her to her feet. She sighed and buried her face in Alasdair's shoulder as he scooped her up, careful not to jar her wing.

.

Chapter 11

THE COOL GOOP Alasdair's sentry had placed on her wing was heavenly. It dulled the throbbing pain, and made it bearable for the male to set her wing in a splint. The specially molded splint would allow her to shift back to human form in a few minutes instead of days.

She met Gideon's watchful gaze from a few feet away. They had helped her into the yard behind the beach house. Outside was the best place. She could stretch out her wing completely so Cassian could mend it. Gideon's brows were drawn together as he stared at her. A sense of uneasiness rolled off him. She sighed and averted her gaze, mostly because she didn't want him to see the hurt in her eyes. She wished there was something she could do to wipe his fears away.

Of course he didn't call them fears, she knew better. His human fear traveled with him into his vampire life. And there she sat, in all her gargoyle glory.

"How's that?" Cassian asked as he moved to stand in front of her.

She carefully flexed her wing, smiling when only a small amount of pain registered. "Good. Thank you."

The gargoyle nodded. "I'd wait a few minutes before shifting."

When he left to go inside, Alasdair stroked her cheek. "That was a very brave thing you did."

Holding up a clawed hand, she shook her head. "I don't run."

A low chuckle left his lips as he took her hand in his. "I wouldn't ask you to, but you do need to work on your aim and controlling your magic a little better." He moved to the side, and ran a finger down the injured wing. She shivered at the feather-like sensation. "I was afraid he killed you at first."

A weight settled on her, heavy and warm. "I miscalculated when I tackled him to the ground. All I could think of was the two of you."

He smiled at her, but it didn't reach his eyes. "I have to speak with my sentries."

"Of course."

When Alasdair left, Rhianna looked out into the dark beach several yards from them. "I must be an ugly monster to you right now."

"The opposite actually. What you did was beyond what I expected." She glanced at him and he cursed. "Shit, sorry. I mean..."

"I know what you meant. I understand... I think." She looked back out to the ocean.

The rustling of his clothes as he moved closer brought her attention back to him. He paced to her, stopping a few inches away. "You are beautiful in both forms."

"You sound shocked to admit that."

"I am."

With great care, she folded her wings into her back, relieved when the injured one complied with only a little pain. She and shuddered as she shifted back to human form. Taking Gideon's face in her hands, she gazed into his eyes, searching for some kind untruth in his words.

There were none. The dark blue depths held nothing but desire.

He's your mate.

Yes, he was. At least one of her mates. Yet, he still hung onto the pain and fear that ended his human life over two hundred years ago. "Being attacked, whether it was by a human or a crazed gargoyle is damaging. Not to mention a horrible way to end one life and enter another. I am not offended if you don't want to see that side me."

He lifted his hand and traced her bottom lip with his thumb. "After tonight, seeing you fight with us, I trust you."

"If I ever start to show signs of going mad..."

"Don't ask me to do it. I already made that promise to Alasdair."

She flung her arms around his waist and hugged him tight. "Then just make sure I never go crazy."

"Done."

"Can I ask you something?"

He gently lifted her head so she met his gaze. "Of course."

"What is Alasdair like?"

His brows dipped, and his forehead creased. "What do you mean? You've met him."

A soft laugh burst free. She tugged out of his embrace. "Yes, but I don't know what he does. Besides I've only been here for one day."

Lacing his fingers with hers, he led her down to the beach. "This is something you should ask him."

"I don't know how to approach him. I mean he seems open, but there's something there I can't explain." She shrugged. "Maybe I'm being chicken."

"Are you afraid of him?"

She jerked to a stop and stared at Gideon. "No."

He raised a brow. "Then what is it?"

"I don't know." She lowered herself onto the sand, and took off her shoes. "I just don't know what to say. If I knew more about him, maybe it'd be easier."

He stretched out beside her, and leaned back on his hands, his legs crossed at the ankles. "It's the bloodlust."

"I wouldn't say it was that completely."

He chuckled. "It's like a purple elephant hovering in the corner of the room. You try to ignore it, but it never really goes away."

"What's he doing about it?"

"Precautions for now. He doesn't feed from humans directly. At first we had a group of humans living here who would donate blood in exchange for free room and board, education, and food." Gideon sat forward, and drew circles in the sand with a single finger.

"I take it that didn't work out because I haven't seen any humans." She watched Gideon's profile he stared out into the dark ocean. The light sea breeze blew through his light brown hair.

He caught her glance out of the corner of his eye and frowned. "No, it didn't. The bloodlust seemed too worsen. The humans were too much of a temptation for him. When blood banks started popping up in the late 1930s, he opened his own."

"I thought Morgan Industries was a pharmaceutical company."

He turned to her then and offering a wide, sensual smile. "It is, to the humans. There are several private medical centers throughout the US for the supernatural beings as well as blood banks for those who choose to use them."

"Makes sense. I never really paid attention to the politics and such. Julian's company is into security for humans and vampires alike." Her father's company was Stone Sentries, Inc., named after the gargoyles that protected the vampire race. Although on the human side, he provided private investigators and bodyguards for high profile clients willing to pay big bucks for security and not ask any questions.

"Yes, I try to take every opportunity to tease your father about his name choice in the company." He faced her and cupped her cheek with his warm hand.

Closing her eyes, she leaned into him, feeling the connection even stronger than before. "Why? Because he named it after the gargoyles? He does have the largest fleet."

His lips lifted in a gorgeous smile. "Only because he's head of security and enforcement for the vampire race."

"True..."

He pressed his lips to hers, ending all her coherent thought. Rhianna groaned, and wrapped her fingers around his biceps, squeezing. Pinpricks of need rushed over her skin and surged through her veins. A hunger like no other consumed her. She let out a soft moan as he swept his tongue in side her mouth, meeting her in a sensually erotic dance.

Gideon slid his hand up her thigh, over her waist, and under her shirt. His fingers tickled as they grazed her ribs. When he cupped her breast, she broke the kiss with a gasp. She met his heated gaze and pushed him onto his back so she could straddle him.

A chuckle escaped him. "A little demanding."

She jerked her shirt off, and peered down at him. "I'm taking advantage of not having to control my strength with you."

"Don't stop on my account." He swept a hand down her arm, and her clothes vanished.

What the hell? "I didn't know telekinetics could do that?"

One brown brow lifted in challenge. "I'm special."

Hmm. She'd have to find out the details later. Right then she wanted the male under her. Without warning, he flipped them over, removing his own clothes with his mind at the same time. "I'm a biter."

A shot of desire burned straight to her pussy. "So am I."

He smiled again, wild and wicked. In that moment she was at his mercy, and she'd gladly surrender to him with the promise of complete bliss. Holding her gaze, he rolled one taut nipple between his fingers, intensifying the ache in her abdomen. With his other hand, he cupped her sex, and stroked slowly. Her breaths came in panting waves as she rocked against his hand. But what she really wanted was for him to be inside her. Now.

"Gideon," she gasped.

Lowering his head, he spoke against her cheek. "So wet. So ready."

"Yes." The single word came out breathless and pleading. Need consumed her mind and her body, making it impossible to think.

He slid one finger inside her, and she bit her lower bit to keep from crying out. When his thumb rubbed her clit, she couldn't hold back. She bucked against him, threading her fingers in his hair, and fisted a handful.

She whimpered when he withdrew his hand, but cried out when he thrust with his cock, filling and stretching her. Fibers of a bond started of weave together in her mind. She knew there were only two things that would allow the bond to start —they truly were mates, and she had accepted him.

She'd felt the connection with him from when she saw him at the coffee shop in New York, then again in her penthouse. The more she spent with him, the stronger the connection. *Shit, they were bonding.*

Gideon froze above her, and stared into her eyes. "What is it?"

"We can't bond without Alas."

"And we won't." He leaned down and kissed before adding, "What you feel is the start. It won't complete until the three of us say the words."

"Oh." She had a lot to learn about mating two vampires.

Gideon pulled out and thrust back in. She moaned and moved against him, letting go of her thoughts. Pleasure swirled inside her, building with each thrust. She scored his back with her nails, and moved in tempo with him. He hissed and met her gaze a moment before he released his fangs. The points sticking out from behind his lips heated her blood, and made her heart race in anticipation.

Yes, please. She clenched her pussy around him. Releasing a low curse, he struck. The sharp sting of the bite only lasted a moment before it was replaced with an overwhelming surge of desire, pushing her over the edge. Release slammed in her, ripping a cry of pleasure from her lungs.

Chapter 12

RHIANNA BLEW OUT a frustrated growl as she slammed another book closed. She'd sat at the round table in the upstairs library for the last three hours, researching curses and Alasdair's family history. There was no surprise that human texts and literature didn't have much information on the family, but she had been able to trace the family name back to a few witches. Nothing else jumped out at her as useful data.

Okay, think Rhi. If she were to curse a journal and hide it, what spell would she use? Dark magic was the first thing to come to mind. She shivered. Dark magic was so heavy and always gave her the feeling of being dirty. However, she would use whatever means she could to protect the vampire race—her adopted race.

Scanning the pile of books and the scattered newspaper clippings spread across the table, she reached for the thick volume of spells she'd found on the top shelf of one of the bookcases. Alasdair had five volumes of them, which she was grateful for. Too bad they didn't come with an index.

She sighed, and opened the book. It was going to take her forever to search through them. It was like finding one needle amongst fifteen haystacks.

"You look tired."

Rhianna jerked her gaze to the tall, yummy vampire filling the doorway. Alasdair wore black slacks and a white button down shirt. "Is that the official uniform for vampire lords?" she teased, thankful for the distraction.

His lips twitched as he stalked toward her. "Just us ancient vampires. The younger ones are a little more rebellious."

She snorted. "Someone is chipper this morning."

Frowning, he scanned the contents on the table. "Have I seemed unhappy to you?"

"Oh, no. I was teasing." She closed the volume of spells and stood. "I sensed so much tension surrounding you. I was surprised you joked back with me."

His vivid blue eyes locked with her gaze, and darkened slightly when he smiled. "I joke with Gideon all the time." He paused and raised his hand to caress her cheek with his knuckles. "I came to take you shopping."

"Shopping for what?" She didn't need anything, and didn't want him to think he had to shower her with gifts to woo her. In fact, she was already starting to fall for them both.

"A Christmas tree…and some decorations," he replied.

Her chest tightened at his sweet offer. "You don't have to do that."

"I want to. Gideon told me you had a tree up at your home."

Averting her gaze, she squashed the bitter ache left by her cheating bastard of an ex-husband. "Old habit from an old life. Really, it's not necessary."

His warm hand cupped her chin and gently lifted it so she met his concerned gaze. "Sometimes it's the reminders of our old life that push us forward to better things."

His lips lifted in a wide smile, warming her heart even more. "Gideon was right. You are a charmer."

"I'll take that as a compliment." He dipped his head and pressed his lips to hers.

The warm sensation around her heart heated, and spread throughout her body. Her panties dampened.

When he broke the kiss, his eyes were a midnight blue. For a moment she thought it was from desire, then he laced his fingers in her hair and tugged her head back, giving him access to her throat. *Shit.* Her pulse raced as she spread her palms on his chest and pushed. There was no effect.

His fangs dropped from his gums and touched her skin. Closing her eyes, she flinched and braced herself. She'd let him bite her, if that was what he wanted. Hell, she wanted it so bad she could taste it. What worried her was his blood lust. What if he couldn't stop? She'd be forced to hurt him. A whimper escaped her before she could stop it.

Alasdair paused, then kissed her neck. "Don't fear me. I can hear your heart racing."

Taking deep, calming breaths, she willed her heart rate to slow and her body to relax. "If you need a taste—"

"No." He pulled back, then put a few feet between them. "I can never take your blood."

Fisting her hands, she glared at him. "Can't or won't?"

"Won't. Not until the mating is complete. Even then there's no guarantee I'll be cured." He started to pace, running his hand through his hair. "The chances I won't be able to stop are too high."

Like hell... She crossed her arms over her chest. "So you don't bite Gideon either? You deny your mate the sensual intimacy other vampires enjoy?"

He snapped his gaze to her. "Gideon is different."

"Why? Because he's a male? Because he's stronger." She crossed the small distance between them and shoved him, sending him stumbling back a few feet. Calling the magic within her, she pushed it down one arm to her hand, then outward for the vampire to see it. "I'm not weak. I have the means to knock you on your ass."

Fuck. Why couldn't she control her temper? She turned away from him and started to clean up the papers and books on the table just to have something to do. The damned vampire struck a major nerve.

"All my life, Julian has protected me and hidden me away." She glanced at him over her shoulder and snarled. "For once, I want someone to see me for what I'm capable of and my strengths and not that I'm a half-breed female."

Her voice trembled and her vision blurred. She didn't want to cry in front of him. *Damn it.*

A moment later, Alasdair slipped his arms around her waist. "I'm sorry. Gideon had to kick my ass and force me to feed from him before I was able to trust myself."

She signed and sagged into him. "I didn't mean to get so angry."

"It is not your place to apologize. If you wish it I can try, but only when Gideon is with us."

Facing him, she cupped his face. "We have to get past our insecurities, if we are to be mated."

His eyes grew round and his lips twitched. "You've made your choice, then?"

"Not so fast." She placed a finger over his lips. "I'm considering it. I feel the pull, but I need to get to know both you better."

"Done." He kissed her. "Now let's go get a Christmas tree."

"CASSIAN LOOKS SO out of place here."

Alasdair laughed at Rhianna's whispered assessment of his sentry. The large, and very old gargoyle looked out of place anywhere.

"He was Annamarie's sentry."

She glanced at him, eyes round in surprise. "Really? He's that old?"

Cassian stepped up behind her, and growled low enough only she and Alasdair heard him.

Rhianna bit her lower lip as if to keep from laughing. "I meant no disrespect, Cassian."

The sentry rolled his eyes and stepped away.

Alasdair swore he saw the gargoyle smile. "Cassian was the one who found my great grandmother in the woods surrounding her home the night the demons attacked."

"Annamarie had a beautiful soul," Cassian said softly.

Alasdair heard the sorrow in the male's voice when he spoke her name. Many times Alasdair wished he could go back and save her.

Sensing the mood dipping, Rhianna changed the subject. "When we go pick out decorations for the tree, I'd like to pick up some wine."

Reaching out, he enveloped her in a hug. "I have wine. You can have your pick when we return home."

"Great." She rose on her toes and kissed him. "I do wish Gideon could come with us."

Alasdair smiled. It had been Gideon's idea to take her tree shopping. The male said it would give the two of them a chance to spend some time together. "Gideon has had his time with you already," Alasdair said.

She frowned. "You're right. I didn't mean... I'm not playing favorites. At least I'm not trying to."

Amused, he stroked her cheek, unable to go very long with touching her. She soothed him in a way Gideon couldn't. "You're not, love. Gideon thought it would be better if we spent more time together. You don't have to worry about jealousy from us. Gideon and I share a bond."

Relaxing, she linked her fingers with his, and started walking again. "Good, because you wouldn't want me to start a schedule."

He threw his head back and laughed. "Gideon and Cassian have me on one enough as it is, I don't need another."

"What about this one?" Cassian asked from a few feet away, gesturing to a large tree.

Rhianna glanced at the male and smiled. The gargoyle stood next to a tree as tall as Cassian's six-foot seven-inch height. The tree was as wide as both Alasdair and Cassian standing side by side. Darting over to the other male, Rhianna studied the tree in awe.

"It's perfect," she said.

"Load it in the truck while I pay for it." Alasdair flagged down one of the attendants working.

"Alas, I can pay for the tree."

"Please, allow me." He offered her a sensual smile that made her drop her shoulders.

"Fine."

He pulled cash from his wallet and handed it to the attendant. Then held out his arm for Rhianna. "Next stop —the department store for decorations."

For the first time since she'd arrived at his and Gideon's home, she appeared happy and excited. He decided he'd do whatever it took to make sure she stayed that way.

Chapter 13

RHIANNA POINTED TO the top of the tree with the hand she held a glass of red wine in. "There's an empty spot."

Glancing from her to the tree, Gideon growled as he walked over to the boxes of glass balls. Holding one of them upside down, he said, "We're all out. Every ornament you bought is on that damn tree."

She tried to pout, but laughed instead. "It's not a *damn* tree." Moving toward him, she stumbled, but Gideon caught her before she fell on her ass.

Taking her glass from her hand, he handed it to Alas. "I think you've had enough to drink."

"Hey, I'm just getting started." She giggled, but focused as best as she could on the tree. Every color imaginable was on the thing. The lights flashed in time to the music. Okay, so maybe it was the wine that made her think they were. They were still pretty, and colorful.

Alasdair came over to stand on her other side. "It's a beautiful tree."

She glanced from one vampire to the other. "So are both of you."

Gideon laughed and scooped her up in his arms and carried her to the sofa. There was a fire going in the stone fireplace. She watched the orange and red flames flicker and listened to the wood crackle while the guys settled beside her. After what seemed like a long silence, she snuggled into Alasdair's chest, and placed her legs in Gideon's lap. Gideon scooted closer to her and Alasdair. "Tell me your love story."

Alasdair glanced at Gideon, who gave him a short nod, before speaking. "Well you know I turned him and why I had to do it."

She nodded, picked up Gideon's hand, and kissed his fingers. "Yes. How did you woo him?"

"It took me some time. He stayed with me for the first year after his transition. It wasn't pleasant. Gideon blamed me for making him a monster. Then there was Cassian. Gideon feared the gargoyle and hated all of them because of what Paris did." Pausing, Alasdair cupped Gideon's nape, then began to message the male's neck. Rhianna sighed at the display.

Clearing his throat, Alasdair continued. "I woke one morning and found Gideon gone. I searched for a whole century before finding him hiding in an alley in town living off animals. That's when I knew I had to use tough love, but I couldn't bring him to Lilith in his condition. She'd rule him a rogue and unfit to continue life as a vampire."

"But didn't Lilith give her permission to turn him?" She couldn't image Gideon as a rogue. He had too pure of a heart.

Alas nodded. "All vampires are able to turn rogue. Anyway, I took him to Julian and left him there."

Rhianna gasped. "Is that why there's so much tension between you and my father?"

Gideon nodded and offered her a half-smile. "He kicked my ass daily."

"It was what he needed to learn what it was to live as a vampire," Alasdair said, a hint of regret in his voice.

Hugging Alasdair, Gideon kissed his temple. "Julian pushed me to discover my strengths in a way Alasdair couldn't. I was so filled with hate and confusion. I blamed Alasdair for cursing me."

"When Gideon was ready he came to me. At first I didn't know if he had come to kill me or not." Alasdair stared into Gideon's eyes and Rhianna felt the love between them. Smiling she waited for Alasdair to continue the story.

"To my relief, he didn't come to kill me, but to seek answers Julian refused him. We drank wine by the fire and I answered every question he had. I also revealed that he was my mate and there was no way I could've allowed him to die outside that church."

Rhianna lifted her gaze to Alasdair. "Then what?"

Gideon answered, "I moved back into the beach house and allowed the vampire to seduce me into his bed."

"I've noticed how good he was at getting me in bed yesterday." She giggled.

A low grow rumbled in his chest. "I get what want."

She yawned. "It's been an exciting day."

Alasdair shifted her body and rose to his feet with her in his arms. "I'm taking you to bed."

"Alas."

"Yes?"

She bit her lip. "Can I sleep in your room?"

In unison and almost instantly, both males said, "Yes."

Laughing, she laid her head on Alasdair's shoulder, and closed her eyes. Life seemed so much less complicated with them. She didn't have to hide who she was and she had two hot ass vampires who'd give her anything she asked. What more could a girl ask for?

Alasdair laid Rhianna in the middle of their bed. She smiled up and chewed on her bottom lip. "I'm not too tired."

Gideon removed his clothes and climbed into bed next to her. "In that case, let us help you undress."

A wide, wicked smile formed on Alasdair's face. With a low growl, he moved the end of the bed and removed her shoes while Gideon worked the buttons on her blouse. Butterflies swarmed in her belly. Sure she'd been with both of them, but not at the same time. Anticipation ran hot under her skin.

Unable to stand how slow they were moving, she reached down to help remove her pants. Gideon gripped her wrist and pinned her arms above her head. Desire flared to life, making her pussy ache.

"Patient, love," Alasdair cooed as he removed her pants, then her panties.

Gideon released her arms so she could slip out of her shirt and bra. Completely bare to them, she bit her bottom lip not knowing what to do next. Gideon dipped his head and flicked his tongue over a nipple, drawing a gasp from her.

Alasdair nipped at her inner thigh and she jumped. Sensations skittered over her warm flesh and her head spun, but it wasn't from the wine she had earlier. Sliding his hand up her leg, Alasdair spread her thighs apart, then licked from her opening to her clit. She moaned and fisted the sheets.

"Watch him," Gideon said into her ear. "He's beautiful."

"Yes," she breathed. No other words would form.

Gideon cupped one breast and rolled her nipple between his fingers while Alasdair teased her clit with his tongue. Pleasure swirled inside her, building higher with every movement. When Alasdair slid two fingers inside her, she gasped and moved against his mouth.

"Come for us," Gideon whispered, his breath warm against her neck. Damn, if she didn't want him to bite her. She tilted her head, and he kissed her neck. "Patience."

Her climax built with each thrust of Alasdair's fingers. Each lap of his tongue made it harder to respond to the other male trailing kisses from her neck to her breasts. Oh, God, they were going to kill her with their passion.

She dug her heels into the bed. Pleasure tore through her as she began to orgasm.

Alasdair trailed feather-like kisses up her body, sending pinpricks of pleasure racing over her. Beside her, Gideon groaned and cupped Alasdair's head, drawing the other male into a deep kiss. A tiny moan caught in her throat at the erotic sight of them together.

Her vampires. Her mates.

She threaded her fingers through each of their hair, raking her nails lightly over their scalps. Alasdair broke the kiss and met her gaze. His eyes were midnight blue and his fangs were poking out from beneath his lip. *Oh yes.* She rotated her hips against him, letting him know she was more than ready.

Gideon stood on his knees, and moved to lean over Alasdair from behind. He put one hand on Alasdair's thick cock and stroked. Rhianna clenched her pussy to ease the ache.

With a growl, Alasdair reached over to the nightstand and picked up the lube. Rhianna's heart pounded as she watched Gideon nip at Alasdair's shoulder and growled, "Don't hold back."

Alasdair frowned briefly, but nodded. He lowered himself, and slid inside her. A soft cry of pleasure escaped her, but she didn't take her eyes off either male. Gideon gave her a crooked smile as he moved his hand to Alasdair's hole, most likely applying the lube before entering the male. The force pushed Alasdair deeper inside, intensifying her mounting pleasure.

They pumped and thrust in unison, rocking her hips. She hooked her feet around Gideon's thighs, needing the feel the connection with both of them as they tumbled into bliss. They increased the tempo, thrusting harder. She shuddered and cried out as her release drove her over the edge. Her males followed in their own releases.

Gideon disappeared into the bathroom, and came back with a towel. After cleaning up, the guys sandwiched her again in the oversized king bed. She let out a sigh and snuggled between them, allowing her lids to drift shut.

Chapter 14

THE MORNING SUN filtered through the blinds, casting thin strips of light across the bed and floor. Rhianna blinked and realized she was alone. Just as she flung the covers off, the bedroom door opened and Alasdair stepped inside holding a tray of food and coffee.

Jumping to her feet, she rushed over to help him, but he sidestepped and nodded toward the bed. "Go sit down. I want to serve you breakfast in bed."

Nibbling on her lower lip to keep a laugh in, she did as she was told. "You don't have to do this."

"Yes, I do. Gideon says I should spend more time with you. Open up to you." One side of his mouth lifted. "So he is handling things at the office today while you and I do whatever you want."

"Anything?"

"Anything."

She thought about it, but the only thing that churned in her mind was the journal and the curse. "I would really like to find out how to break the curse on the journal."

He unfolded the small legs from under the tray and placed it over her lap, then sat beside her. "So would I, but we can do that this evening when Gideon returns."

He was right. Plus, it'd be a lot faster if the three of them worked together. "Okay. So what is there to do?"

He lifted the lid from her plate and she stifled a greedy moan. The sugary sweet scent of French toast and berries drifted into the air. Her stomach growled as if telling her to hurry the hell up and eat. As she picked up her fork and took the first bite, she noticed Alasdair watching with interest.

"Do you play golf?" he asked.

She frowned, and shook her head. "No."

"What about boats?"

"I love boating. It's so relaxing." Lifting her gaze to his, she smiled at the spark of joy lighting up his eyes.

"Good. Finish eating while I go tell Cassian to make the arrangements. Then he left, not giving her any time to ask questions about what he had planned for her.

But that was Alasdair. Take charge and make arrangements before, then deal with the details later. Julian was pretty much the same way, but Alasdair had a more laid back approach. For the first time since arriving, she realized how much Gideon and Alasdair were alike. It was a good thing, because she was already half in love with Gideon.

Half in love? No, that wasn't right. She was falling for the vampire at rapid speed. *Please dear Lilith, I hope Alasdair and I can form a bond.* If not, she'd suffer a broken heart that could kill her gargoyle side and leave her human side damaged as well.

ALASDAIR HELD HIS hand out to assist Rhianna onto the yacht. She allowed him to help her aboard, all the while scanning the boat. When she returned her gaze to his, she smiled.

"This is amazing."

"Thank you. It's like my home away from home. Gideon and I take her out often to escape." It'd always felt like he was calmer when he was out in the middle of the gulf —no one around but a Gideon, and a sentry.

Rhianna faced him and narrowed her eyes slightly. "Escape from what?"

He shrugged and led her into cabin. The high for the day was supposed to be around sixty-five degrees, but with the boat in motion it would feel a lot cooler. "Being on the water is soothing. It's almost like my bloodlust is muted."

With her gaze still on him, she drew her brows together as if in thought.

"What?" he asked, sensing her unasked question.

"Just something Gideon mentioned the night before. He said your bloodlust started a few months after you two committed to one another. Do you remember if it was gradual, or did it start up suddenly?" She asked as she dug her smartphone out of her bag and started scrolling through some kind of ebook app.

"What are you doing?"

She glanced back up at him. "One thing that bothers me about your *illness* is that you haven't passed it onto Gideon."

"It takes time for the sickness to develop."

She shook her head and went back to scrolling on her phone. "Not necessarily. In Gideon's case, his anger from being turned without his knowledge would've triggered it, but he fought his whole nature and refused to feed."

Shit, she was right. Not feeding regularly would've brought on the bloodlust. "What if my illness isn't genetic?"

"I believe it's not. I also believe it's not the kind of bloodlust most rogues fall to." Rogues are labeled as such because they broke laws of secrecy and over-feed on humans. Their cravings are fueled by power and control, and not the need for blood like the born illness.

"Then what do you believe?" he watched her tap her screen and turn the phone for him to see.

"A magically enhanced potion."

He narrowed his gaze at the small screen. "How would they get me to take a serum without my knowledge?"

She lowered the phone and shrugged. "My first guess is your blood supply."

He folded his arms over his chest, but before he could say anything, she continued. "Gideon told me you haven't fed on humans since you started developing signs of bloodlust. How much do you trust your lab techs?"

"Explicitly."

"Are you the only one in the house who drinks the bagged stuff?"

Doubt settled in. He was the only one who had blood delivered to the house. What would inducing bloodlust in him accomplish? "I'm not seeing the "why" behind it. Plus Carlos, the tech in charge of my blood, is a vampire with no magical qualities about him."

"Someone could be giving him the serum. As for why, I can only guess to throw you out of your lord status. Who would be lord over your territory if something happened to you?" Her brows dipped as her forehead creased.

"Gideon," he answered.

Shaking her head, she began to pace. "No. That's not it then. They'd need to take care of him as well, unless they are counting on you killing him in a bloodlust induced rage. But that doesn't make sense either." She stopped and glanced at him. "I don't understand why they would keep you battling the effects for over a hundred years."

He took her face into his hands, forcing her to make eye contact with him. "I'll text Gideon and have him check some things out at the lab while he's there. You and I are supposed to be relaxing and getting to know each other."

The corners of her lips dipped into a frown. "I don't want you drinking anymore blood from the lab."

"How will I feed, then?"

"From me."

His mind screamed no as she placed a finger over his lips.

"Ask Gideon about his little tap he got at my penthouse. If I believe for one second that you are out of control, I am more that capable of stopping you."

"Even if it meant hurting me or possibly killing me?"

"Yes, but only because I know you'd beg me to." She looked him straight in the eye.

He snaked an arm around her waist and jerked her body to his. "How can you be so sure?"

"I can see your soul through your eyes. While you fight the need for blood on a daily basis, you still hold onto what makes you... you." She flattened her palm on his cheek. "I know in my heart that you could be a mate for me."

He lifted a brow. "There's a "but" in there."

She sighed. "I'm confused. Gideon and I—"

"I know. You've bonded. Or started to." He kissed her on the lips softly.

"That doesn't bother you?"

Smiling, he nipped at her nose. "Just the opposite. It excites me. Tells me we are closer to forming a triad."

"But why is it so important?"

"It's what is fated to be. I saw you in a vision before you were born."

She drew her head back and stared. "So you two have had the last fifty years or so to get used to the idea?"

He smiled. "Seventy-five." When she opened her mouth to speak again, he placed a finger over her lips. "It's more than a vision. It's a feeling of completeness. Of knowing there is another out there for the both of us."

"No jealousy?" Her chocolate gaze stared at him for several moments without blinking.

He chuckled. "You've spent too much time with humans. Vampires can be very possessive. If a male besides Gideon were to touch you, I'd kill him."

She laughed and glanced down as she fingered the top button of his shirt. "No matter how much this doesn't make sense to me now, I can't walk away. My gargoyle and I are curious about you."

He hesitated, focusing on her full lips for a moment, and then tugged her to sit on the sofa. "What has you so curious?"

Sitting back, she hesitated for a few moments. "What's your favorite color?"

"Green."

Her brows kitted together and her nose crinkled. "Why green?"

He laughed. "Is it odd for me to like the color?"

"No. It just took me by surprise. I would've thought it was blue or red."

"My mother's eyes were green."

A smile lit up her face. "That's sweet."

With a finger over her lips, he leaned in and nipped at her nose. "I'm very old and boring. I work too much and care a great deal about my vampire family. My loyalty is to Lilith and my mates."

With one finger, he lifted her chin and claimed her lips, stopping her questions. When their lips touched, sensations swarmed him, raising a raw desire from deep inside. She moaned, an almost pleading sound, and wrapped her arms around his neck. He gripped her waist when she shifted to stand on her knees, and then straddled his lap. Their tongues tangled as their mouths meshed together. She tasted of mint with a slight rose note. His body hummed and every caress ignited the growing flame of desire. He slid a hand under her shirt and up her back, drawing a slight shiver from her.

With his other hand, he twined his fingers in her hair and pulled as he trailed kissed down her jaw to her throat. He hesitated, feeling the rush of need for the blood flowing under her skin beneath his lips. Her heart beat thumped, teasing and enticing him to bite.

She gripped his hair tighter and tugged him closer. "Please...don't stop."

"Clothes. Off." His voice was rough like gravel.

Her sweet rose scent sharpened, indicating her arousal had spiked. She scrambled off his lap and undressed. When she took a step forward, he dipped his head and covered her sex with his mouth. He tucked an arm under one warm, silken thigh and lifted. She grabbed ahold of his shoulders and dug her nails into his skin. The sting of her nails heightened his need to possess her. Desire and pleasure mingled and grew until he could no longer think. He slid his tongue into her folds, making her cry out.

He draped her leg over his shoulder, and inserted two fingers inside her. He teased her clit with his tongue as he pumped his fingers in and out. Her pussy tightened and she cried out just before she came in a shuddering orgasm.

After making sure she was steady on her feet, he stood and removed his clothes. When he met her stare, he smiled and looped an arm around her waist, tugging her flush against his body.

"You're beautiful."

Her cheeks turned a bright pink and she averted her gaze as if his compliment embarrassed her. He lifted her chin with a finger and kissed her lips softly.

"You're our mate."

"I know," she said with an assurance in her gaze that sparkled.

"You've accepted it." It wasn't a question, but more of a challenge.

One corner of her lip lifted. "Mostly."

"Don't tease me female." He tapped her on her ass, making her squeak.

The half smirk turned into a wicked grin right before she pushed him onto the sofa. "I can tease if I want." She straddled him, hovering her pussy over his cock. "It only makes the finale even better."

She took him in her hand, and he hissed at her warm touch. When she eased down, taking all of him, a passion like he'd never felt heated his blood and raced throughout his body. He gripped her hips, and moved her up and down, slow at first, and then faster until they screamed their release together.

Chapter 15

THE THREE OF them sat in the study with a volume of spells. Rhianna had given Gideon and Alasdair keywords to look for while they scanned through the books. The counter spell for the journal should have something to do with changing languages or shifting words. She'd also told them to look for anything to do with letters or words.

Yet, they'd been in the study for five hours and hadn't found a single thing.

"What if it has nothing to do with language or words?" Gideon said, breaking the silence.

Rhianna blew out a breath. She wished she knew what curse was used to scramble the words in the journal. "I'm not sure what else it could be."

Alasdair leaned back in his chair and stretched his arms over his head. "What are we looking for again?"

She let out a huff, but Alasdair smiled, halting her from spatting out what she'd been thinking.

He held her gaze for several moments before speaking. "So maybe we're thinking about this all wrong. Why aren't we looking for a spell to convert the words back to English?"

"Because the journal was cursed and it changed when I arrived here."

Gideon made a noise. "But that doesn't make sense. It was supposed to be hidden from Violet and the demons, not Alasdair."

He was right. None of this made sense. *Unless...* "Do you have any demons living in the house or on the property?"

"Just a few echo demons in the guest house." Alasdair narrowed his gaze, then shook his head. "They have been with me for over a century, and I've never had any problems from them."

Echo demons were created and bred by Lucifer for the sole purpose to serve the high lords of hell. When Lilith came to the human realm, she freed the earth side echoes and deemed them under her protection. Anyone who mistreated them in any way would be punished, unmercifully. Most echoes lived with and served vampire lords or Lilith herself.

Rhianna stood, picked up the journal, and walked to the door. "I want to meet them."

"The echoes are peaceful beings," Alasdair protested as he stood.

"Yes, I know. Some of them are known to become witches' familiars in exchange for shelter and food. Julian has several on his staff." She sighed. "I believe you might have a spy living in the house."

Gideon stepped out the door and waited. "A spy?"

"Yes. It makes more sense as to why the curse activated. The magic used is dark and very powerful. Only a priestess or warlock priest is strong enough to perform the ritual to ensure it lasted this long. I don't think it was you who caused it to reactivate." Rhianna followed Gideon down the stairs.

"But why did it deactivate?" Alasdair said from behind her.

Rhianna thought about it for a moment. "I don't think it did. But I'm just thinking out loud and I'm not a hundred percent. New York is a Violet free zone. Julian and the gargoyles make sure of it with the help of a coven of witches within the city."

Gideon let out a low growl. "There must be six families of gargoyles living in the area. Any demon to step foot in Julian's region is either stupid or has a death wish."

Laughing, Rhianna corrected his guess on the number of sentries in New York. "Actually there are fifteen families in the North Atlantic region."

"Another reason I hated the area." Gideon faced her when he reached the ground floor, a half smile stretching one side of his mouth.

Rolling her eyes, she stepped aside to allow Alasdair to lead the way to the guesthouse on the Oceanside of the house. Her stomach knotted and her palms clammed up. The echoes at her father's home had always been uncomfortable around her.

When they reached the small cottage-style house surrounded by palms and sand domes, she hesitated.

Gideon glanced at her, his brows drawn together. "What is it?"

"Echoes are uncomfortable around me. I just don't want them to be afraid of me."

Holding out his hand, Gideon smiled, melting her heart a little more. "Then this should be fun."

Alasdair snorted. "Gideon, behave. The echoes will be fine." He knocked on the door.

A young female opened it instantly. She had white-blond hair hanging to her waist, lavender colored eyes, and a button nose. Rhianna guessed the girl was no more than fifteen.

The *echo* smiled wide at Alasdair, then Gideon, but when her gaze met Rhianna's the young demon frowned and started to shake. "My lord?"

Alasdair took the girl's hand in his. "Cyn, this is Rhianna, Gideon's and my mate."

Cyn visibly relaxed and nodded at Rhianna. "I'm sorry. Welcome."

Rhianna offered her hand. "Hi. No worries. My father's echoes have never even made eye contact with me." The girl looked confused, so Rhianna added, "Julian Delacroix is my adopted father. He raised me from an infant."

An older version of the girl appeared behind her. "My lord? Please come in."

The older *echo* wasn't upset by her presence like her daughter had been. Rhianna knew something was off. The demon didn't fear her, was deliberately not making eye contact, and was only speaking to Alasdair and Gideon. At least her father's echoes would speak to her if they were in the same room, even if they were shaking with fear.

"Judy, meet our mate, Rhianna." Alasdair's tone had a slight warning in it as he spoke. Rhianna wondered if he too had sensed the cold shoulder act.

Judy turned her gaze Rhianna and forced a smile. "Welcome."

In her arm, the journal grew warm and tingles of dark magic bit at Rhianna's skin through her thin long sleeve. *Interesting.* "Thank you. Is it just you and Cyn who live here?"

"Oh no, my mate and son are at one of the covens in Miami. His sister gave birth to her second child." Judy motioned to the couch and chair. "Please have a seat. I'll make some tea."

An odd sense that something was wrong rose up within her, setting her gargoyle on edge. She clenched the book tighter and glanced at Alas, then Gideon, who was watching her with intense interest. She mouthed, "Later," to Gideon.

He moved closer to her and ran a finger down her arm. She sighed and leaned into him. When he dipped his head to nuzzle her neck, he whispered, "A lot of tension in this room."

She couldn't agree more, and she'd be glad when they left and returned to the main house so she could fire off the mounting questions to Alasdair.

When Judy returned to the living room, she set down a tray with a teapot, cups, and sugar. Rhianna inhaled. The black tea smelled of jasmine with a hint of mint.

"It smells wonderful."

Judy smiled and poured everyone's tea except hers and Cyn's. If it was anyone else, Rhianna would be suspicious, but echoes didn't eat or drink with their lords unless asked to. To Rhianna's relief, Alasdair motioned to the tea with his cup. "Please drink with us."

More tension left Rhianna as the female poured two more cups of tea. *Seriously, Rhi, you are being paranoid.* Taking a sip, she smiled. "This is good. It's been a long time since I've had really good tea."

"Thank you, Miss." Judy took a drink of her own before asking. "You are the new mistress of the house?"

"Oh, not yet. I'm still thinking about it." Rhianna loosened her hold on the book and laid in her lap. Judy watched the movement, eying the journal as if she wanted to grab it and run out the door.

Suddenly, Gideon stood. "Thank you for the tea, Judy, but we must be going."

Rhianna stood beside him; so glad Gideon had picked up on something. She wasn't sure if it was the same thing she had, nor did she care. "Yes, thank you. We should get together soon when I have more time to spend with you."

When she sent a pointed look to Alasdair, he pursed his lips and stood beside them. "Have Daniel call me with updates on the baby."

"I will, my lord." Judy smiled, set her cup down, and stood as they left the guesthouse.

Once inside the great room of the main house, Alasdair whirled around to face her and Gideon. "What the hell is wrong with you two?"

When Gideon didn't speak right away, Rhianna rushed out, "The journal reacted to Judy."

Shaking his head, Alasdair paced the room. "Not possible. Judy has been with me since she was a child."

Taking a deep breath, Rhianna crossed the room, took Alasdair's hand, and placed it on the journal.

He flinched at first, then stared at the book. "Nothing happened."

"Then my theory is correct. The curse is not directed at you or this house. It protects the book from demons who have ties to Violet." She pushed the book to Alasdair until he held in his hands. "Open it."

He did as she asked. His forehead creased as a frown formed on his lips. "I can read it." he snapped the book close. "I can't accuse her without proof. She's like family. Hell, her whole family had been loyal to mine since Annamarie was turned."

Rhianna moved closer and rested a palm to his chest. "I know. I hope she isn't the one who triggers the curse."

"One way or another, we can't ignore it." Gideon dropped onto the sofa and blew out a breath. "I can't see why she would betray you, but if she is... the reason has to be life or death."

Rhianna bit her bottom lip. The compassion the vampires had for Judy made her stomach knot up with guilt. However, Rhianna couldn't dismiss her intuition.

"I'm so sorry, but I'm hardly ever wrong about these kind of things."

Alasdair met her stare, sadness hid in the blue depths. "I hope you are wrong this time. Especially for Cyn's sake."

So did she. Her nose started to tingle and her chest tightened at the thought of the young girl losing her mother. Even though Rhianna had Bless, the gargoyle wasn't the mothering type on her best days. Many times Rhianna wished she'd had a mother to hold her. Pushing the feelings aside, she walked into Alasdair's arms and hugged him tight.

"So do I."

VIOLET PACED THE small space of the two-bedroom apartment she temporarily shared with Wyn. It was the best they could do on short notice. Destin, Florida was a fucking tourist town, and every hotel and beach rental was booked with humans seeking a warm climate.

The door opened, drawing her attention to the male entering the apartment. "Well?"

Wyn lifted his gaze to her and smiled. "It is done. My spy has given the potion to Alasdair."

Her lips lifted into a smile. "Good. I was afraid the female would back out."

A chuckle escaped Wyn as he paced to her. "Not if she wishes to see her boy again. I'm confident she will obey since I killed her mate. Then I threatened to take her daughter and sell her to the highest bidder in Hell."

A spark of excitement lit up inside her. Threading her fingers into his hair, Violet pulled his head back, baring his neck to her. "I love it when you talk about torture. My sister will get what she deserves for having me cast out of Lucifer's bed."

Wyn growled. "You are too good for any of them, my queen."

"Yes. Together, my love, we will rule the human realm. Then we'll claim Lucifer's throne in the underworld." She would succeed one way or another. Even if she had to kill Lilith to do it.

Chapter 16

ALASDAIR'S VISION BLURRED for a brief moment. A wave of dizziness washed over him. His fangs elongated and his stomach cramped, making him double over. *Fuck. Not now. Why now?*

He hadn't had an attack since Rhianna arrived. Stumbling to the small fridge in the corner of his study, he pulled out a bag of blood and popped it to his teeth. Once the bag emptied, he jerked it from his fangs and growled in frustration. His stomach still ached. In fact it seemed to be getting worse. Unable to fight the need, he left the study and climbed the stairs. The house was quiet. *Too fucking quiet.* Where the hell was Gideon?

He reached the top of the stares and caught Rhianna's rose scent. His dick hardened behind the zipper of his jeans. Following the smell of rose water, he entered the library and focused on the female curled up on the sofa with a book.

She raised her head and smiled. Just as quickly as it formed, the smile faded. "Are you feeling okay?"

No. "Yeah. Fine. Where's Gideon?"

"He and Cassian went to get a smaller tree and decorations." She laughed softly and set her book down. "I mentioned that it'd be nice to decorate the library and, well... you know Gideon."

He relaxed a little, but didn't move from the doorway. "Do you need anything?"

"No. I was about to get a bath, but I got caught in a book." She stood and stretched.

He groaned and his fangs throbbed. *Damn it.* Maybe he just needed release. It helped before with Gideon. Then again Gideon would take control and make him force the bloodlust away. "When Gideon returns can you send him to my study?"

She cocked her head to the side and folded her arms. "You're aroused." She advanced toward him. "And battling your bloodlust right now. How bad is it?"

His whole body shook. "Don't."

"How bad is it?" she asked again a little firmer.

"The worst I've ever experienced." There was no use lying to her. She was a witch, she'd know if he lied.

She moved closer until she was only inches from him. He closed his eyes and held his breath. When she cupped his cheek, he flinched but didn't move. She rose to her toes, and nipped him on the chin. "Tell me what you want."

He groaned and walked her backward until her back flattened against the wall. Her scent clouded his mind, intensifying the need to possess every inch of her. A groan escaped her before she wrapped her legs around his waist. His skin heated as pleasure washed over him. Rhianna ripped his shirt open and pressed her palms to his chest.

A low growl escaped his lips, and pressed his hard cock into her. *Too much clothing.* He needed her bare. He lowered her to her feet. "I need you naked."

She met his stare, and lifted her lips before removing her clothes. Another growl rumbled from his chest as he captured her mouth in a deep kiss. He cupped her ass and lifted her off the ground again, pressing her back to the wall. With one quick movement he thrust inside her, drawing a gasp-turned-moan from her.

Her arms wrapped around his shoulders, and she fisted her hands in his hair as she rode each thrust. Her moans changed to cries of pleasure as her pussy clench him. His body tensed and his balls tighten right before an orgasm slammed into the both of them.

RHIANNA'S BODY FELT boneless, as she lay draped over Alas. She could still sense his hunger and see it in his eyes. Multi-shades of blue swirled around his elongated pupils. His fight to resist his urge to feed didn't go unnoticed.

"Why didn't you take what you needed from me?"

He tensed, and refused to look at her. "I will not use you to curb my cravings."

What the fuck was he talking about? She pushed up to hover over him, her anger growing with each word. "First, I am one of your mates. Second, you need to trust in the fact that I'm not afraid of you. I can knock you on your ass if I have to. We talked about this already."

He met her gaze, grabbed her upper arms, and moved her to the side so he could get up. "I will not take your blood while I'm fighting bloodlust." He backed away a few steps.

She stood and stormed over to him. Poking him in the chest, she let out her frustration. "I refuse to be shut out. This affects all of us, not just you." Letting out a deep sigh, she softened her tone. "Let me help you until we figure out what's causing it."

"No." He stepped back and she reached for him, but he darted out of the way, snatching up his jeans as he left the library.

Rushing to the door, she went to the railing and peered over. He was gone. Her eyes burned as the tears began to fall. It was too close to a rejection.

Why wouldn't he trust her?

Chapter 17

THE DAMP NIGHT air nipped at Alasdair's skin as he walked down the beach in hopes of wearing himself out, or at least until he calmed down enough to return and talk with Rhianna. He couldn't understand what got into him. Bloodlust had never hit him that hard before, and he'd never gotten angry.

What if she was right and someone at the lab put something in his blood? Then there was the possibility that Judy was working with Violet. He had to find some answers.

The sound of people talking brought his attention to a large sand dune he'd just walked past. Ducking behind some cattails, he was surprised to hear Judy's soft, pleading voice.

"I did everything you asked. Can I at least see him?"

"Not until I'm sure that witch and her vampire lord hand over the book."

Alasdair didn't recognize the male's voice. His chest tightened. Rhianna had been right. *Damn it.*

The scent of sulfur and dirt coiled around him, tingling his nose. With a low growl, he whirled around and bared his fangs at the two demons charging him from behind. Alasdair darted to right, dodging one of the bastards while at the same time clothes-lining the other with his arm. Pain exploded in his chest as electric currents shot through his body in convulsing waves. He glanced down and cursed at the taser probes sticking out of his chest. His body shook uncontrollably as he fell to his knees.

His vision blinked in and out and his heart rate increased. Judy's cries for help were cut off abruptly, and he hoped they didn't kill her. One of the demons crouched beside him right before Alasdair felt a sharp stick to his arm. He tried to regain control over his arms and legs, but failed as darkness consumed him.

GIDEON CARRIED THE five-foot tall Christmas tree into the library and froze at the salty scent of tears. He spotted Rhianna at the small round table with all the volumes of spell books open. A box of tissues sat within her reach.

Carefully he set the tree down and approached her. "Rhianna, are you okay?"

She sniffed. "Yeah, just fucking peachy."

Okay, so he'd take that as a hell no. "What happened? Where's Alas?"

"Gone."

His heart dropped to the floor. "What do you mean?"

She took a shaky breath. "He was having a bad episode and I offered to help, he got mad or spooked or something. Anyway, he left out the back door."

Okay, calm down. That was easier said than done. Gideon had a sick feeling that something was wrong once he walked through the front door. "How long ago was that?"

She lifted one shoulder. "About thirty minutes ago, I think."

Panic rose again. Alasdair never went anywhere without Cassian, but the gargoyle was with Gideon. Alasdair should've been back by now, or sitting out back. Gideon grabbed Rhianna's hand and tugged her out of the library and down the stairs.

"Where are we going?" she protested.

"To find Alas." They exited out the back door and scanned the yard and the beach. No sign of him. *Fuck.* "He wouldn't just leave. No matter how pissed or upset he was."

"Gideon!" The panicked cry from Cyn made him whirl around to face the *echo.* Her eyes were red, and her cheeks soaked with tears. He rushed to her. "What happened?"

"Mom. Demons." She sucked in a sob. "They took them."

Gideon drew her into a hug. "Start at the beginning. Who took who?"

"Demons. One came to the house and momma went outside to speak with him. I don't understand why she'd do that." She pulled back to meet Gideon's gaze. "Why would she talk with him?"

Glancing at Rhianna, his heart sank. By the frown and watery eyes, he knew Rhianna did as well. Returning his attention back to Cyn, he cupped her face and forced her to look at him. "You said they took *them*. Was Alasdair there too?"

She nodded, eyes wide and lips trembling. "They shot him with a Taser before they teleported away."

Fuuuck. He stood and took Cyn's hand. "Violet has them," he growled out as he led the girl into the house.

Rhianna followed. "What will she do to them?"

Once inside, Gideon sat Cyn down on the couch and faced Rhianna. He was on the verge of exploding. His skin was too tight. His chest ached, and he wanted to destroy something, or someone. He'd never experienced so much violent intent in his life. With each second that passed, his need to kill something grew.

"Violet will torture Alasdair until he gives her the book. Hell, she may just do it for fun until we show up. I'm not sure what she'll do Judy."

"Then we'll take her the book."

"No!" Gideon cursed when she winced at his harsh tone. He reached out for her and spoke in a slightly softer tone. "We can't give her what she wants. Alasdair wouldn't want it that way."

She pulled out of his reach and clicked her tongue. "She won't be able to read it. Sure, she could know how to break the curse, but that will still take time. We use that time to get Alasdair and Judy out of there. With all of us we could grab the book and leave."

Cassian's heavy boots pounded on the floor as he crossed the room. "She's on the right track, but I agree about the book. We can't allow the demon bitch anywhere near it."

"Then we make a fake one."

Gideon stared at her and then gave a nod. It could work. A fake journal could distraction Violet for a little while. "How will you do that?"

She held out her hand, palm up. A swirl of magically charged energy formed over her hand, then vanished leaving behind two identical looking books. She handed him the top one. He took it and frowned. "That's the journal you bought yesterday."

"It's similar enough to Annamarie's journal that I shouldn't have a problem crafting the duplicating spell." She set the real journal on the coffee table before crouching down in front of Cyn. "Do you know where you father and brother are?"

Cyn glanced to Gideon, then Cassian before returning her attention back to Rhianna. "My father is dead."

Gideon pressed his lips tighter, not liking where this was heading, but he remained silent and watched how calm Rhianna was with the girl.

"You know this for sure?"

Cyn nodded, a tear rolling down her cheek. "I feel it." She tapped her chest over her heart. "Peter, my brother, is alive, but I don't know where."

Of course. "That was the leverage Violet used to get Judy to work with her."

Rhianna nodded and spoke to Cyn. "Would you like to be my familiar and help me locate your mother and Alas?"

Cyn hiccupped and nodded. "Anything."

"Good." Rhianna stood. "Run up to my room—it's the one next to the master suite—and get the black wooden box on the dresser."

Without hesitation, Cyn darted off to do as she was told. Gideon grabbed Rhianna by the upper arm and drew her closer. "We don't have much time."

"It will take less time, if both spells can be crafted at the same time. The binding ritual between me and Cyn will only take a minute." She hugged him tight. "I want him home safe as quickly as possible."

Gideon rubbed her back. "He's strong and stubborn as hell. We'll bring him home."

And make Violet and her demonic minions pay for taking him.

Chapter 18

RHIANNA SET HER ritual box in the middle of the coffee table, opened it, and pulled out a piece of white chalk. Gideon and Cassian had moved the furniture from the middle of the great room, giving them space to work.

She handed the chalk to Cyn. "Take this and draw a circle around us. Make sure it is big enough we can move around the coffee table if we need to."

Cyn took the chalk and began outlining. Rhianna pulled out some sage and two white candles. Breaking a small amount of sage off, she placed it in a small copper bowl and lit it, letting it burn for a few moments before blowing the flame out. Picking up the bowl, she walked along the inner edge of the circle, then crossing through the middle.

"May this circle be clear of all negative energies."

Meeting Cyn in front of the coffee table, Rhianna set the bowl down and picked up a small knife. She gazed into the girl's eyes and smiled. "I need you to slice your palm. Not too deep, just enough for the blood to bead to the surface."

Cyn nodded and did as instructed, and then handed the knife back to Rhianna, who repeated the act. Rhianna held her hand up, palm facing Cyn. "Press yours to mine." When the girl obeyed, Rhianna linked their fingers. "Do you, Cyn, wish to be my familiar, aiding me in all things magical as well as services I may call upon you in the future?"

The echo's eyes grew round, and Rhianna tightened her hold on the girl's hand. Their linked palms warmed and began to tingle where their blood was mingling. Rhianna had expected it, but knew Cyn wouldn't have.

"Cyn, focus on my face and voice. The warmth from the magic will spread and circle around us. There is nothing to fear. Do you understand?"

The girl nodded, tears pooled in her lavender eyes, breaking Rhianna's heart. Poor thing had lost her father and possibly her mother and brother. Swallowing the lump stuck in her throat, Rhianna continued. "Do you pledge your loyalty to me? And understand that this is an unbreakable bond?"

"I do." Cyn took a deep breath and straightened her back while never breaking eye contact with Rhianna. "I trust you and will aid you in whatever you need from me."

Good girl. The bond was going to be a strong one. Power wound around their linked hands like invisible ribbons soaked in hot water. It coiled around their arms, spreading until it surrounded them completely. The magic hugged them as if it had arms.

Cyn shifted her gaze, but Rhianna touched her cheek, drawing the teen's attention again. A moment later the magic expanded outward, then the energy snapped back, slamming into them. Rhianna gasped, gripped Cyn's hand a little tighter, and pulled her into a one-armed hug.

"You okay?" Rhianna whispered in the girl's hair.

Cyn nodded. "That was intense, but I don't feel any different."

Releasing a sigh of relief, Rhianna let go of her. "You're not supposed to, not really. I mean you'll feel a slight tug on your conscience when I call large amounts of magic. Other than that, you are and will always be you."

When the *echo* nodded, Rhianna picked up her wand from the box as a powerful dark energy snapped through the room. Rhianna stepped in front of Cyn and crouched, preparing for the worst. Gideon and Cassian simply turned around. *What the hell?*

The males stepped aside, and Rhianna's heart dropped to her stomach. Lilith approached, her ice blue eyes fixed on the journal. Dressed in a black gown that matched her raven-colored hair, the vampire queen glided across the floor as if she floated.

Rhianna bowed, and lowered her gaze. "Your majesty."

When Lilith reached her, she held out a hand. "Don't be so formal with me. We don't have time for it." She glanced at Cyn. "You agreed to the binding?"

The *echo* nodded, refusing to look up.

Rhianna tugged at the girl to stand next to her. "I would never force a familiar binding on anyone."

Lilith returned her attention to Rhianna. The queen stared for a long moment before speaking. "I know. I was just testing the child to see if she knew what she got herself into."

"I would do anything to save my mom and brother, my queen." Cyn spoke so softly Rhianna almost missed it.

Lilith heard it though.

Instead of replying, Lilith picked up the journal from the coffee table and then the one Rhianna bought. The queen held a book in each hand, and closed her eyes. A flash of white light made Rhianna jerk back. Once the spots cleared from her vision, she noted two identical books, and not from any spell she could cast.

"Amazing. How do we tell them apart?" Rhianna picked the one on the right, the one she purchased. It was identical from the crest on the cover to every worn spot on the leather.

"Go ahead and open it."

Rhianna obeyed and shook her head. "This is far better than I could have done."

Lilith tucked the real journal into her robes. "My sister would've sensed the spell as soon as you got near her. She will not be able to pick up on this spell until it is too late."

"Too late for what?" Rhianna glanced to her.

Her lips curled and her gaze darkened. "It will dissolve about two minutes after she opens it."

Gideon stepped forward. "We must be going."

Rhianna turned to Cyn and frowned. Lilith touched her shoulder. "Go. I'll stay with Cyn."

Shoulders sagging, Rhianna turned to follow Cassian and Gideon out the door. Cyn didn't need a babysitter, but Rhianna was relieved to know she wouldn't be left to follow them—something the teen was likely to have done otherwise. Lilith wouldn't let that happen.

Rhianna didn't have time to worry about Cyn. She had to take her mate back and find Cyn's family. Violet had messed with the wrong female.

Chapter 19

GIDEON YANKED AT the chains and roared. "Fucking Violet. Show yourself, bitch."

Beside him, huddled in the corner of the concrete cell Judy sobbed and whispered over and over, "Please forgive me my lord."

As much as he wanted her to be quiet, he couldn't yell at her. No, this whole fucked up mess was Violet's doing.

"Judy," he gritted out, wincing when he voice came out a graveled wreck. "Judy, please focus on my voice. We'll get out of here and find Peter. Violet won't get away with this."

Another sob sounded before she fell silent. He sighed. "Do you understand me? I need your help." Glancing at her, he saw her uncurl herself and slowly stand. "I need blood."

When she took a step toward him, his fangs dropped and the dizzying need of bloodlust slammed in him. "Stop!"

She whimpered and rushed back to the corner. "My lord?"

Inhaling through his nose, he pushed the dark cravings down. "Not you. Call for the guards tell them you know where the journal is. Beg them if you have to. Whatever it takes to get them to open the door."

Violet had injected him with some kind of serum. The affects were hitting him hard and he recognized the symptoms from those at the house the night before, after he drank Judy's tea. A low growl escaped from him. Violet would pay for forcing his *echo* to betray him.

"Go on, Judy."

She scrambled to the door and spoke through the small window of bars. "Guards. Please, don't make me stay in here. The lord...he is mad. Please. I lied. I know where the journal is. The witch has it."

Alasdair growled loudly at the reference to Rhianna. Judy cried out and banged on the door. "I'll do whatever Violet asks to help expose Lilith to the humans."

Good girl. Alasdair rested his head against the stone wall behind him and waited. Judy's voice trembled, but he couldn't tell if she was frightened more of him or Violet. Maybe it was both of them.

A few moments later one of the large demon guards came to the door. "Step back."

When she did, the demon unlocked and opened the door. That was Alasdair's cue. He roared and snapped his teeth at the male. The demon snarled as he entered and snapped a whip at him. The sting of the braided leather across his chest only fueled the mounting anger and bloodlust. With a jerk, he strained against the chains, pulling them until they snapped.

Alasdair bared his teeth, and charged the demon. He took him down and buried his fangs in the male's shoulder. The demon's scream echoed off the dungeon walls, but Alasdair was too far gone to care. Warm blood flowed down his throat, only soothing the hunger a little.

The male went limp under him and a moment later his heart stopped. Alasdair rose to feet and met Judy's wide eyes. He shook his head. "Come. The others will be here soon."

She rushed out the cell door and led him through the narrow maze of hallways. After what seemed like forever, they reached a door. Judy went to open it, but Alasdair placed a hand over hers. Holding his finger to his lips, he listened —the sound of boots hitting the stone floor made Alasdair growl. Someone was coming.

He pushed Judy behind him and crouched. When the door opened, he froze. Cassian filled up the doorway, his long black hair pulled back into a ponytail. The gargoyle raised a brow, but smiled. "It's good to see you too, my lord."

"Likewise. Where are my mates? I can smell their scents on you."

Cassian paused and let out a soft curse. "They will be with us soon."

Alasdair growled. "Where are they?"

"Should be in Violet's chambers—"

Alasdair didn't wait for the gargoyle to finish speaking before he pushed his way past him. He'd be damned if Violet hurt his mates.

RHIANNA'S HEART POUNDED as she and Gideon entered the large room where Violet's demon guard took them. The plan was for her to be seen coming onto the property. Gideon was supposed to go with Cassian to free Alasdair, but the stubborn vampire refused to leave her side.

The room wasn't what Rhianna had expected. Although she'd wasn't sure what to expect from the queen of demons, but a conference style room wasn't it. The large horned demon leading them turned to her, gripped her upper arm, and not-too-gently sat her in a chair. Gideon let out a growl that shook the windows.

When the demon advanced on Gideon, Rhianna shot out her hand and placed a circle around the asshat.

The bastard snarled at her. "You will pay for that, female."

"Shalom, you will not harm the witch."

Rhianna jerked her attention the door as Violet entered. Like her sister, she too had long midnight black hair. Unlike Lilith, Violet's eyes were dark blue and void of compassion. Even though both were demons with powers that at one time rivaled the high lords of hell, the females were polar opposites.

"I guess you would like to have that pleasure," Rhianna bit out as she stood.

Violet's gaze darkened before she focused on the book cradled in Rhianna's arms. "Give me the journal."

"Not until you free Alasdair and the *echoes*."

An evil laugh burst from the demon queen. "You try to bargain with me? I think not."

Violet lunged for the book, but Rhianna darted out of the way, overturning chairs as she moved with her gargoyle super speed. Gideon rammed into Violet's side, sending both of them into the wall, leaving a large hole in the drywall.

A tug on Rhianna's conscience told her the demon was trying to break out the circle she'd put him in. *No you don't.* With a flick of a hand her, she closed a second circle around him. *That should hold him for a little while longer.*

Gideon let out a painful roar.

Rhianna focused on Violet and called the element of fire. Since she was an earth witch, she could connect to the elements. The magic heated and spiraled inside her, growing as she opened her mind and called to the element lords.

Gathering the power into a tight ball in her chest, she pushed it out to her hands. Her fingers tingled and for a moment she thought her hold on the fire slipped. Then a boost of power burst from her, engulfing her hand in blue and orange flames. Her familiar had to be helping her, but how could Cyn boost that much power?

Suddenly Lilith's icy mint scent filled her awareness right before the vampire queen's voice entered her mind.

Don't question the bond's strength. Finish it.

IT'S A VAMPIRE CHRISTMAS

Focusing a glare on Violet as the bitch faced her, eyes round with shock. "It's over Violet." Rhianna thrust her hands out, throwing the flames straight at Violet, but they didn't make contact. The cowardly bitch teleported away a moment before the blast hit her. The fire consumed the wall behind where had been, swiftly spreading through the room and out into other parts of the building. *Fuck.*

Rhianna rushed over to Gideon. "You okay?"

"Yeah. We need to find the echoes and Alasdair." Gideon grabbed her hand and tugged her out of the room. In the hallway, they ran into Alasdair. Rhianna almost cried her relief.

Alasdair enveloped her in his arms and buried his nose into her neck. She hugged him back, while very aware his bloodlust rode him far worse than earlier. It would take time for the potion Violet had given him to run its course. They'd have to deal with that later.

"Where's Cassian?" Rhianna pulled back and searched Alasdair's face.

"He took Judy to go find Peter. They will meet us at home." He glanced to the fire quickly moving through the building. "We need to get the hell out of here."

Rhianna nodded and allowed her vampires to rush her out. She couldn't wait to get home —her new home in Destin, Florida with her mates. "When we get things settled with Judy, I have a surprise for both of you."

The males stopped a few yards from the building and looked at her. Alasdair was the one who spoke with a knowing smile. "You've made your choice."

LIA DAVIS

"Yes, and I chose both of you. I love you both and want to complete the bond."

Gideon scooped her up in his arms and ran to the car. "Come on, Alas, we have a mate to please."

The vampire lord laughed and followed them. "Yes, love. We'll please her every night for the rest of our existence." Once at the car door, Gideon gently placed her in the front seat before he climbed in the back. Alasdair cupped her cheek. "I love you. I've loved you since before we met."

Her chest tightened and she kissed him. "I think I have too, I just didn't know it. Take me home."

Epilogue

GIDEON BURST THROUGH the front door with Carlos, the lab tech from Morgan Laboratories, by the collar and dropped the traitorous vampire on the floor in front of Alasdair. Letting out a growl, Gideon spoke through his teeth. "Tell you lord what you told me."

Rhianna's gaze bounced from male to male, her heart beating like a scared rabbit from the electricity of the emotions running through the room. They suspected Carlos had been spiking Alasdair's blood with a serum that enhanced the cravings of blood. Looks like the vampire had confessed, or Gideon had beaten the information out of him.

Alasdair raised a brow at Carlos, waiting for the male to speak.

With his head low, Carlos spilled. "I'm responsible for putting the serum in your blood."

"Why?"

Carlos lifted his gaze to Alasdair. "Because Violet will free us all. No more rules of secrecy. The vampire race will be at the top of the food chain where we belong."

Rhianna fisted her hands and forced herself to stay in her seat when she wanted to get up and snap the bastard's neck. No one messed with her mates. Ever.

As if sensing her anger, Gideon stalked over and sat beside her. "He's not worth it."

Alasdair growled, low. "Cassian!" When the gargoyle entered the room, Alasdair motioned to Carlos. "Take him to Lilith."

Cassian snatched up the low-life and dragged him out the door. Rhianna met Alasdair's gaze as he crossed to room to her. "I wanted to snap his neck."

He flashed her a brilliant smile. "Yes, so do I, love, but his punishment will be far more painful with Lilith."

True.

She studied her vampire lord for several moments. He looked healthier than he had when she arrived three weeks ago. "So what are we going to do today?"

Gideon chuckled and Alasdair's eyes flashed midnight blue. "You are going to give us your decision."

They didn't know? "You going to make me say it?" she teased.

Alasdair leaned down, caging her in his arms. "Oh, yes. After you say it, we're going to complete the bond and fuck you until you can't stand for a few days."

"We plan to hold you hostage and have our way with you over and over." Gideon ran a finger up Alasdair's arm.

She sighed dramatically. "Well, you know you can't hold someone hostage if they're a willing prisoner."

Alasdair growled, igniting desire inside her. She cupped his cheek with one hand and Gideon's with the other. "I love the both you and want to be your bonded mate."

She let out a squeak as Alasdair scooped her up and carried her toward the stairs —Gideon hot on his heels. Laughing, she buried her nose into his neck and inhaled. Her heart was filled. She'd never dreamed of have a true mate, but the Fates had given her two.

Life was a crazy, beautiful thing, and she was the luckiest witch alive.

The End

ABOUT THE AUTHOR:

Lia Davis is a mother to two young adults and three equally special kitties, a wife to her soul mate, and a lover of romance. She and her family live in Northeast Florida battling hurricanes and very humid summers. But it's her home and she loves it!

An accounting major, Lia has always been a dreamer with a very active imagination. The wheels in her head never stop. She ventured into the world of writing and publishing in 2008 and loves it more than she imagined. Writing is stress reliever that allows her to go off in her corner of the house and enter into another world that she created, leaving real life where it belongs.

Her favorite things are spending time with family, traveling, reading, writing, chocolate, coffee, nature and hanging out with her kitties.

FIND OUT MORE ABOUT LIA DAVIS HERE:

Website: http://www.authorliadavis.com
Newsletter: http://eepurl.com/mBWx5
Facebook: https://www.facebook.com/lia.davis.52
Facebook Fan Club:
https://www.facebook.com/liadavisfanclub/
Twitter: @novelbylia

IF YOU ENJOYED
IT'S A VAMPIRE CHRISTMAS,
TRY THE MAGICAL WORLD OF GREEK
GODS AND DRAGONS IN LIA DAVIS'S
SONS OF WAR SERIES!

READ ON FOR AN EXCERPT...

I

A COLD SENSATION rolled down Gwen's spine like an icy finger as she stepped out onto the back porch of her parents' Florida home. She focused her senses out into the cool evening, and inhaled the fragrance of night jasmine lingering on the breeze. The moonless, star-filled sky didn't chase away the feeling of menace lurking in the shadows, waiting. The awareness had clung to her since she'd woken that morning and she wished she could feel the creatures of the night like her best friend and adopted sister, Elle, could. Although Gwen descended from the gods themselves, sensing monsters wasn't her gift. As the great-granddaughter of Nyx, goddess of the night, Elle could see into the darkness and all her secrets.

Descended from the goddess of love, Gwen held the power of persuasion, and she could sway people, especially men, to bend to her will. The gift came from her father's side of the family—Tom Preston was one of Aphrodite's earthborn sons.

She loved nights like this as well as the calm that blanketed the small town of Perry. It was a few minutes before midnight and everyone slept. Elle had left early that morning to show her latest paintings and sculptures at a gallery in Jacksonville. It was the first time the girls had been apart since becoming friends in the third grade.

The sound of glass breaking behind her made Gwen's heart hammer and her stomach clenched. Spinning, she saw three large men charge into her home through what used to be the front door. Splintered wood lay half in the kitchen, half in the living room, and the long rectangular windows on either side of the entrance were destroyed. Glass littered the living room floor.

Fear rushed through her like wildfire and she darted to the side to hide behind the curtain of the sliding glass door. Helplessness consumed her as she watched one of the men open drawers to her father's desk, dumping the contents on the floor. Another searched the living room, then stepped into the kitchen. Her heart sank as the third man turned toward the hallway.

Mom, Dad.

Without another thought for her own safety, she rushed after the man that went down the hall. Before she could make it, another man crashed into her, slamming her to the ground. Sharp, stabbing pain shot from her hip down her leg. Gwen screamed, hoping to wake her parents, as she clawed at the man's face, aiming for his eyes.

A loud thump followed by her mother's cry reached Gwen's ears. Terror filled her, cold and crippling. Tears ran down her cheeks. A moment later the man that went towards her parents' room flew backwards through the living room, and further until he crashed into the kitchen island. Then her father stood at the hallway entrance, hands fisted by his side.

"Let her go."

Gwen stared at her father in disbelief. His body glowed with power.

"You think to use mortal magic on me?" The man holding her laughed, then released Gwen and rose to his feet.

A bright flash of black and gold light filled the room, leaving a large black dragon where the man had been. Disbelief and horror twined through her veins as she stared at the creature. Smoke rolled out its long snout and the eyes almost glowed red. Shaking, she managed to scramble backwards to keep from being trampled by the beast—which was way too big for the house.

Her father held his hands out from his body, palms facing the dragon. A soft white light beamed from the center of his hands, then brightened and grew into a ball of bright white energy the size of cantaloupe before her father thrust it at the dragon.

Gwen screamed again, not knowing what she could do. There was a freaking dragon inside her home and her father...well, she didn't know what he threw at the beast because he'd never used his magic to that extent before. The ball of light didn't do anything, but drive the dragon back a step and whip his tail around to hit Gwen. The blow knocked her out the back door. Landing on the deck, she watched in horror as the dragon breathed fire toward her father.

Tears streaming down her face, she shouted for her father to get out, but too late. Flames covered him and he stumbled forward, igniting the carpet with each step and the couch as he fell. The dragon let out a roar that rocked the house. The men that came with him rushed outside right before the beast blew out another blast of fire and swiveled his head around the room. The whole house engulfed in flames within seconds.

Agony ripped through Gwen's heart and she sobbed, but no one heard her.